Glimmer

An Anthology of Hope

Edited by

Sef Churchill

and

Justin Boote

Silvery Press

Copyright © 2020 Justin Boote, Sef Churchill

All rights reserved.

These stories are works of fiction. Names, characters, places, and incidents either are the products of the author's imagination or are used fictitiously. Any resemblance to actual persons, living or dead, businesses, companies, events, or locales is entirely coincidental.

ISBN: 9798583338658

CONTENTS

Dedication: Des Dixon	i
No Experience Needed – Cathy Ryan	1
A Time to Dance – Joslyn Chase	8
Hunger – Justin Boote	17
Hope 2020 – M. C. Dalton	23
Silence - Gary Little	32
Long Range Transmission – Sef Churchill	40
Who Wants To go For a Walk? – Iseult Murphy	50
The Returning – Edmund Stone	57
Rituals from Beyond the Grave – Antonia Juel	66
Cero Miedo – Ryan Benson	76
Night Scar – W. E. Pearson	84
Deeper than Love – David Rae	90
Six Steps Forward - D. A. Steen	98
The Terminator Line – David Safford	114
Hope in a Bowling Alley – Carole Wolfe	128
When the Carnival Came to Town, and Two Poems – Theresa Jacobs	134

The Rained-on Reindeer - John King	148
A Crack in the Sidewalk – Monica Mackinnon	156
10 Microfictions – David Ratledge	165
Infinite Blue – Ken Carriere	168
A Woodstock Wish – Des Dixon	177
Family – Des Dixon	184
The Dinosaurs – Evie Haskell	185
A Wake No Longer – J. H. O'Rourke	190
Unconditional – J.H. O'Rourke	191
About the Authors	200

GLIMMER

DEDICATION

For Des Dixon

To the curator of Canadian war tales, the creator of Cade Cannon, and the kind and clever critique partner, thank you for your words and your humor. - David Safford

Thank you Des for sharing your stories! Your writing made me smile! Every time I see a fedora, I'll think of you! – Jennifer Kelly

Des... You made me smile every time I saw a post, comment, or opened an email from you. You spoiled me with encouragement and gratitude for the smallest things. I'll miss you, dear friend. - Callie Sutcliffe

Des, your humor was one of a kind, I'll never forget you. You'll forever live in the pages of Cade Cannon for me, every time I read it, I'll think of you. - Edmund Stone

Des, your name will live on through your writing, and your heart will live on through every one of us you touched. - Theresa Jacobs

Des, you never failed to touch my heart and put a smile on my face. I love your stories and greatly enjoy reading about your family, the Canadian Air Force, interesting and inspiring historical events, and - of course - Cade and Camilla.

Your limericks and poems have tickled us here at TWP and your influence is far-reaching and will go on. I'm very grateful that you published some of your work before you left us and I'm proud to have it on my bookshelf.

Thank you so much, Des. We'll miss you! - Joslyn Chase

Ah, dear Des. What a bright light he was. He will.be missed. He was a testament to what a writer should be...one who never gives up. Age can't stop you. Fear can't stop you. Writer's block can't stop you. Criticism can't stop you. Only God can take away our last breath. I'm sure he's up there in heaven writing away and telling his stories. May he rest in peace. - Wendy Pearson

He was a good guy. Glad he got Cade Cannon published. He was proud of Cade. His stories about his early years, WW 2 and what life was like then were his best works. RIP, old friend. – Joe Arcara

You were one of a kind. My days are more interesting after reading your words and happier having known you. You will be missed, Des. -Ryan Benson

Des had a way with words in his quirky stories and critiques along with a wonderful sense of humor. He was my friend and I will miss him. He always made me smile. -JH O'Rourke

In Memoriam - Des Dixon 2020

The room, hollow and empty,
The chair, empty and sagging.
A sadness fills the air.
Curtains billowing,
lightly caressing a single key.
Sitting and waiting for that touch,
A screen brightens.
A cursor sits and blinks,
ending a thought,
ending a book,
ending a story.

   - Gary G Little

GLIMMER

NO EXPERIENCE NEEDED
Cathy Ryan

Larry, fourteen and tall for his age, stood in Mr. Franklin's kitchen with his back to the door. He clasped his hands behind his back, fingers intertwined and wringing. Mrs. Cleveland, beside him on his left, was arguing with her father, Mr. Franklin, who was seated at the kitchen table facing them. Momma had taught Larry it was not polite to listen to other people's conversations so he tried not to listen. It was hard though because they were kind of loud.

Mrs. Cleveland had told Larry on the way over that there was only so much time she could spare from her job and volunteer work to maintain her father's household while he recovered. She'd brought Larry to help.

She yelled at her father, "For once, why don't you think about someone other than yourself." She did an abrupt about-face and stomped out of the house, leaving Larry alone with Mr. Franklin. The flimsy screen door slapped shut behind her and Larry flinched at the sound.

"I don't need any damn help!" Mr. Franklin yelled loud enough to be certain his daughter heard him as she crossed the porch. The sound of her heels clacked away without a moment's pause.

Mr. Franklin hadn't risen when Larry and Mrs. Cleveland arrived and he didn't stand now. He panted with fury and glared at Larry who stood between the table and the kitchen door. "Take this boy with you!"

Larry sighed. His grandma had been angry sometimes,

too, before she died. Mr. Franklin reminded him of her in that way.

Larry realized Mr. Franklin even had the same kitchen set as Grandma's. The table had a slick white rectangular top with rounded corners and a two-inch band of chromed steel around the edge. The table legs and chairs were tubular steel. His chairs had thick cushions on the seats and backs, covered in blue plastic. Grandma's were red. One of hers had a crack in the seat, too, with white cotton batting showing through.

Outside, Mrs. Cleveland slammed her car door, started the engine, and drove away. She had warned Larry that her father might not be receptive at first, but he'd come around she'd said, if Larry was persistent. For Larry, this was the job he needed. One he could do after school and weekends.

A black and white collie lay under the table. Ears up, he watched Mr. Franklin and thumped his tail. Larry shuffled his feet and waited. Silence grew between the man, the boy, and the dog. The dog laid his head down on the carpet and sighed.

"What d'you know about cattle?"

Larry flinched. Mrs. Cleveland had assured Larry the cattle were out to pasture. They had water and a neighbor was checking on them and the fences daily. She knew he hadn't grown up on a farm like all the other kids around here. The only thing he knew about cows was that they were big. He didn't like them. "Nothing. Sir."

The man shouted. "Then what the hell are you doing here?"

"Mrs. Cleveland said you wanted help around the house." Indoor help, she'd said. Like what he'd done for Grandma. Larry shifted his eyes toward the kitchen sink filled with dirty dishes and the cluttered countertops. Mr. Franklin was recovering from a stroke, but Larry wasn't supposed to mention that.

"You know nothing about cattle. What the hell good are you to me?"

The boy looked down, swallowed. He knew how to clean up and do laundry and read medicine bottles.

"Answer!"

"I, I, I -- she said you'd tell me."

"What!"

"What you needed."

"I don't need anything!"

Larry could sweep floors and take out the trash. He eyed the trash bin so overfilled the lid had fallen upside down to the floor beside it and was now hidden under discarded frozen food wrappers. The dog stretched a long quivering stretch so his toenails rattled on the table leg, then he settled flat-sided to sleep again.

"Can you drive a truck?"

Larry shifted his eyes sideways. He had driven a few times in a parking lot, but whenever he got near another car his mother would scream and grab the wheel. Out here, he wasn't likely to be near other cars. "A little," he said.

"A little. You'll be my chauffeur, then. Always wanted a God damn chauffeur."

The boy blushed. The work was all supposed to be inside. That's what she'd said. She said Mr. Franklin couldn't go out.

"You don't like it when I say, 'God damn?' Ms Sunday school teacher should have warned you."

Mrs. Cleveland was a Sunday school teacher. That's how Larry met her. His grandmother took him to church when he visited. After Larry and his mom moved in with Grandma, he got to know Mrs. Cleveland better.

Mr. Franklin began to pry himself into a standing position. It was a long, slow process. "You can drive me out to the cattle."

Larry's eyes widened in alarm. To do what?

Mr. Franklin rocked and swayed and grabbed for the back of his chair. Hands outstretched, Larry stepped toward him. He knew about helping that way, too. Mr. Franklin glared. "Don't."

Larry froze.

"Close your mouth." He shifted his grip on the chair and clutched the cane hanging there, then turned and began to hobble from the kitchen to the living room. 'Come,' he growled. The dog and the boy both followed through the living room where the floor was strewn with newspapers, socks, and a rawhide dog bone. A wire waste basket beside a leather recliner overflowed with tissues. An E-Z reach gripper like the one Grandma had used was on the floor next to the wastebasket. Plates were stacked on the other side of the chair. Larry glanced at the dog. Those plates looked licked clean.

They reached the front door and Mr. Franklin pulled it open. He staggered and righted himself. A brown, Ford pickup truck with rusted fenders was parked at the foot of the front porch steps.

Wide-eyed, Larry watched the old man teeter his way toward the first step of four. The dog raced to the bottom and stood waiting beside the truck with his tail swaying, jaws agape, tongue lolled.

Larry rushed down past Mr. Franklin, turned at the bottom, poised to break his fall if necessary, and watched in breathless fascination as he crept down.

Mr. Franklin took the final step and Larry opened the truck door. The dog jumped inside. The old man gripped the door frame with one hand and threw his cane across the seat. He clutched the front of the seat with his left hand and put one foot inside. He paused there and swayed. Larry, twitching with anxiety, almost gave him a boost, but didn't dare touch. Finally with a growl and grunt, the old man hoisted himself inside. He panted from the effort. "Shut the door."

Larry took a hasty glance for fingers and toes and slammed the truck door.

"The house door, you idiot!"

Larry raced back up the steps, drew the house door shut, took a deep breath, and ran down again.

He paused at the driver's door. This was crazy. What was he doing? Mrs. Cleveland had said he didn't need to know anything about farm work. He would cook, clean, help her father get around the house, play card games, and read to him. Those were all things he had done for his grandmother.

This wasn't fair. Mr. Franklin wasn't supposed to even go outside. What if he fell down out there or the truck quit working? Neither one of them had a cell phone.

"Excuses!" He practically heard Grandma's voice crack at his ear. She hated excuses.

But what if he had to walk back for help, walk back through the cattle herd? His gut twisted. Chicken. He was afraid.

So what? This wasn't what he was promised.

Back in February, after she died, Grandma's Social Security check stopped coming. Money had been tight before and now there was less. Larry wanted to get a job then to help out but Momma said 'no.' "I could quit school. Get a GED," he said.

"No," she said. "You will go to college. We'll make do."

Momma never missed a day of work herself. Not before Grandma died, and not after. She never did. Afterward, she grew thinner and thinner, though. One night, Larry got up in the night and found her crying. She'd been opening the mail. Even with one less mouth to feed, they couldn't pay the rent. That's when Larry realized she had not been eating in order to save money.

He got a work permit that let him work around school hours. Fair or not, afraid or not, Larry needed this job. If only Mr. Franklin would have him.

He opened the truck door. On the driver's side behind the steering wheel, bits of dirty cotton stuffing poked through the torn seat. He grabbed the steering wheel and pulled himself up.

The dog had his front paws on the dash and stared out the windshield. His tail swept gently back and forth. The old man stared out the windshield, too, his mouth in puckered silence.

There was a shifting lever on the column and three pedals on the floor. Three. Larry's heart sank. His mom's little hatchback had two. He pushed the brake down, and wobbled the stick shift. He paused a moment, then turned the key. The truck lunged forward and stopped.

The old man leaned back and glared across the dog. Sweat trickled down Larry's temple. He tried it again. Foot on the brake, turned the key. The truck jumped forward and died.

The old man spoke. "Never drove a stick shift." His voice was flat, slow, precise with no hint of a question.

"No, sir."

"Hell of a chauffeur."

Larry swallowed. If Mr. Franklin told him to leave, he'd have to walk home. It was only five miles. He'd planned to ride his bike over after school each day. The dog panted. His front paws tap-danced on the dash. The windshield fogged from his breath. One drop of drool landed between his paws.

"D'you see that pedal on the left?"

Larry nodded.

"Speak up, boy! D'you see it?"

"Yes, sir."

"Put your foot on it."

Larry did.

"That's your clutch. D'you see the one in the middle?"

Larry nodded. "Yes, sir."

"Put your other foot on it."

Larry did.

"Now turn the key."

The engine started.

Mr. Franklin talked Larry through learning to coordinate the clutch and gas pedal, easing the truck forward, and then stopping and shifting and easing backward in reverse. He never raised his voice once and Larry began to feel hopeful.

"See that gate over there?" Mr. Franklin said. "Let's head

over that way and look at the cows."

Larry's heart began to pound again. He opened the gate, drove through, closed the gate behind them and restarted the truck engine without a hitch though and Mr. Franklin said, "Good job."

"You're not from around here, are you?" he asked and Larry told him about the city where he and his mother had lived before. They found the cattle herd and watched the cows eat grass for a while then returned to the house.

Larry followed Mr. Franklin inside. "D'you want me to clean up a little?" he asked.

Mr. Franklin settled into his recliner before he answered. "Maybe tomorrow, after school. How are you getting home, son?"

Larry thought of how his mom would smile when he handed her his pay.

*

Cathy Ryan enjoys writing, gardening, and playing piano. She lives on a small farm in Virginia with her husband and a cat. The cat supervises both writing and gardening and leaves the house during piano practice. Cathy (not the cat) has short fiction appearing in 'Beneath Ceaseless Skies' and the anthologies 'Deep Waters' and 'Once Upon a Story.' She is revising her first novel. Visit her website to see more of her work. https://cathyryanwrites.com

A TIME TO DANCE
Joslyn Chase

The world knew how to somersault, and it was doing it again.

Gisele Ngono paced the tiny confines of her Phoenix apartment, redolent with fried onions from last night's dinner and stuffy, despite the open window. She'd hardly stepped foot from the place in weeks except to gossip with neighbors in the courtyard, everyone maintaining the prescribed distance and speaking through the gaily-printed masks Gisele had produced from her second-hand Singer.

Life had been in a holding pattern, but with the bloom of spring—the fragrant popcorn buds on plum trees out front, the buzz of waking insects—came the hope of renewal. Gisele had been looking forward to pushing the reset button, getting back to normal.

That was before the phone call.

With a shaking hand, Gisele clutched the mobile before putting it down again, a cold lump forming at the back of her throat. She tried to ignore the baleful message, but knew it must be dealt with. The call had come while she was in the shower, a summons from Ms. Bonaventura, owner of the design agency where Gisele worked. It couldn't bode well. The terse message had ended with a command to return the call.

Gisele padded across the worn carpet and stepped onto the pitted linoleum of the kitchen floor, feeling its texture against her bare toes. She opened the refrigerator, surveyed two cartons of raspberry yogurt, a dried-out chicken breast, and half a lemon, deciding she wasn't hungry. Too restless to sit, she paced through the small apartment, fingering the cheap fabric of the curtains, straightening books on the shelf she and her roommate had made from cinderblocks and plywood.

She'd been in much nicer apartments since her arrival in the States but this place, humble as it was, met her needs and she was grateful to have it. For the time being, she had it to herself. When Corona gripped the nation, her roommate, Sandra, had gone home to ride it out with family, leaving Gisele alone. Almost everyone in Gisele's own family was either dead, missing, or still in Cameroon.

Gisele dawdled as long as she could, inventing aimless tasks like sorting through the stack of quarantined mail, cleaning grunge from the window runners, and swirling the scrubber around the toilet bowl—again—until the task could no longer be avoided. Ms. Bonaventura was expecting her call.

Even after two years working in the design department, Gisele still feared the formidable woman who ran the place. Impeccably dressed, every perfectly-tinted hair in place, she stalked the halls with breezy impunity, making people dance with the point of a finger. Her eyes frightened Gisele most of all—steely gray, piercing and pitiless.

George had laughed when she told him this. "No, you've got it all wrong," he said. "Karen's remarkably shrewd, that's all."

Lifting the phone, Gisele gripped it hard, determined to follow through this time. She entered the number and hit SEND. The call connected instantly and Gisele swallowed hard, wondering what to say. It was a needless worry.

"Gisele," Ms. Bonaventura said, her cold voice showing no sign of ice-breaking small talk. "I wanted to speak with you about tomorrow's meeting, nine o'clock. It's time we resumed full-scale operations."

"I'll be there, Ms. Bonaventura," Gisele promised.

"Good. I've had some time over the lockdown to evaluate and there will be some changes coming. George, for instance, won't be with us anymore."

The cold lump in Gisele's throat plummeted to her stomach. "What do you mean, Ms. Wester—"

"I've got another call coming in. I'll talk to you tomorrow. Nine sharp."

The phone went silent. The cold lump in Gisele's stomach threatened to exit forcibly. She went to the open window and leaned against the sill, gulping down big breaths of pollen-dusted air. The sound of twittering birds filtered in around her, their carefree song a mocking accompaniment to her deepening anxiety.

She didn't know what was happening—the meeting, the changes, George—but she did know one thing:

The world, in all its somersaulting, was getting ready to roll right over her.

*

Gisele stared at the three tubes of lipstick she owned. Which shade would best convey confidence without screaming audacity? Which brand was most likely to still look fresh when her mouth had gone dry? Grimacing at herself in the mirror, she swept them all into her case.

At the end of the day, would it really matter what shade of lipstick she'd been fired in? And besides, half of it would end up smeared on the inside of the mask she was required to wear on the bus.

She left the apartment early, giving herself an hour and a half to make the twenty-minute commute. With the reduced bus schedule and social distancing restrictions, who knew how long it might take? As she waited at the bus stop, she agonized over George, still struggling with what he'd told her over the phone last night.

"I just talked to Ms. Bonaventura," Gisele told him, unable to keep the dismay from her voice. "She said you're not coming back. What did she mean, George? Will you be at tomorrow's meeting?"

There was a pause before George spoke, sounding tired. "I won't be attending, Gisele, because I'm sick."

"Oh, George—say it's not Covid!"

"Don't fret, Gisele. I'm okay. I don't have any of the risk factors so I'm sure I'll make a quick recovery, but I'm in quarantine. That's why I won't be at the meeting."

"But after you're well—you'll be back then, won't you?"

The pause was longer this time, and Gisele felt her misgivings multiply. "I've decided to retire," he said at last. "Working from home has given me a new perspective and I think it's the right thing for me to do."

Trying to keep a selfish whine from sneaking into her voice, Gisele said, "Okay. Then I'm happy for you, George, if that's what you want."

He laughed. "Don't sound so worried, Gisele. You'll be fine without me."

"No I won't," she wailed. "Without you, I'd still be pumping out a daily quota at the sewing machines."

"You've never stopped doing that," he said. "Granted, it's a more refined quota, at a more advanced sewing machine, but Karen will always get her money's worth out of you."

"She doesn't like me," Gisele insisted. "She only gave me a chance at design because you talked her into it."

"Me, and all my charms. Look, Gisele, you've got to stop thinking like that. You've got talent. I got your foot in the door, but it's up to you to dance."

The rumble of the approaching bus roused her back to the present. A squeal of brakes, and the bus pulled to a stop in front of her, the doors thumping open.

"I'm sorry, miss," said the driver. "You'll have to wait for the next one. We're full."

Gisele looked through the windows of the bus. In Cameroon, every seat would be jammed, with a chicken in each lap before the driver called it full. Here, she saw whole rows of empty seats.

The driver shrugged. "I'm sorry, social distancing, you know."

He swung the door shut and the bus lumbered off. Gisele checked her phone. She still had plenty of time, assuming she could get on the next bus. She waited, thinking about all the buses she'd boarded in her flight from Cameroon to Ecuador, passing through Colombia, Panama, Costa Rica, Nicaragua, Honduras, Guatemala, and Mexico before finally reaching the United States.

Her cousin, Vanina, had made a similar journey a year prior, and was working on gaining American citizenship. She'd written to Gisele with instructions, encouragement, and an address where to meet her in Phoenix when she arrived. It had taken Giselle more than six months to complete the trek, and when she finally reached the address Vanina had given her, no one knew what had become of her cousin.

Alone, disheartened, and utterly destitute, Gisele had wandered the streets, ending up at a shelter where they gave her a bowl of hot soup and the name of a social worker. After a series of small miracles, Gisele found a job sewing piecework for Ms. Bonaventura's design house and moved into the tiny apartment with Sandra.

Remembering how happy she'd been just to have a job and a place to lay her head, Gisele tried to tell herself life was still good. But in truth, this felt like the worst day since leaving Cameroon. The piecework job had been fine at first—she hadn't really minded the monotony and the crick in her neck. But moving up to the design department, having a hand in planning and creating the fashions, small as her contribution had been, made it hard to think about going back to the basement room filled with rows of sewing machines and utter drudgery.

Or worse, she could lose her job altogether.

Another bus chugged up to the curb, its back doors folding open with a bang. Gisele, and half a dozen others, boarded, careful to keep a wide space between them. It wasn't until ten minutes down the road that Gisele learned the route had been shortened, leaving her with an eight-block hike on foot. The buffer of time she'd left herself was narrowing swiftly.

Terrified of being late, Gisele rushed along the city streets. Despite the warm Phoenix morning, a chill shuddered through her at how deserted the shops, office buildings, and sidewalks appeared. This had once been a teeming thoroughfare, now only dotted with passers-by, anonymous behind the masks they wore.

Gisele thought again about her first days in the city, forlorn and frightened. In the sewing room, there had been little talk, every head bent over a pile of work, and Gisele had been lonely. George's was the first really friendly face she'd encountered there.

He'd passed her station, carrying an armload of skirt panels, but stopped, backing up to peer down at her stitch work.

"What are you doing there?" he asked, pointing to a slight modification she'd made to a dart design.

Afraid of what she'd done, Gisele floundered, trying to find words to explain, but George dropped the skirt panels to the floor and pulled a notebook from his pocket, thrusting a pencil at her. "Draw me a picture of this dress, how you think it should look." he demanded.

Frightened, Gisele had drawn the dress as she envisioned it. She didn't have the whole pattern, didn't know what the finished product was meant to look like, but she did have a picture of something in her head and she drew it for George while he stood looking down at her, a smile slowly stretching across his face.

He'd taken the paper from her and disappeared, leaving the skirt panels heaped on the floor. The next day, he'd welcomed her into the design department where she'd been given a place at the table and a few small jobs on the team. It was because of George that she'd moved up from the basement, and without him, Gisele feared a return to the basement was what Ms. Bonaventura meant by saying there would be some changes coming.

The dreary surroundings, the cut in pay, these would make her sad, but the real bitter part of the pill would come in losing the chance to share her skills, to contribute as part of a team, to create something lovely and see it develop from start to finish. Gisele realized how happy she'd been during these last two years.

And now Covid was taking all that away.

*

At last, the building which housed the design firm came into view, and Gisele ran, glad she'd chosen to wear low, sensible heels. She imagined sweat stains forming underneath her jacket—not the sort of fashion statement Ms. Bonaventura's house of design would appreciate. Passing a bank's digital marquee, she saw it was already two minutes past nine, and she remembered the dark look Ms. Bonaventura had given her on the only other occasion she'd been late to a meeting—a look that said, "You're not making the cut."

If the woman was looking for reasons to justify sacking her, Gisele had just given her one more.

Heart pounding, legs trembling, Gisele opened the door to the conference room. She hurried toward her chair, an apology on her lips, and stopped solid as if hitting an invisible wall.

The table was massive, large enough to allow distancing between the meeting's participants, but her chair—the place where Gisele belonged—was occupied. A stranger sat there, a woman Gisele had never seen before, vapor rising from a ceramic mug of coffee, sketches scattered across the notebook in front of her. Comfortable here, fitting in.

For a long moment, Gisele stood frozen, fighting the heat of unreleased tears beneath her faltering eyelids. Nor did she move when Ms. Bonaventura spoke, introducing the new designer.

Already it had happened, so much sooner than she'd hoped. Where was she to go? Back to the basement? Onto the street to find a new job? Without George here to promote and bolster her, she was nothing.

Ms. Bonaventura's eyes, sharp as ever, drilled into Gisele. Some of the designers at the table had chosen to wear masks, but the boss's face was bare, leaving nothing to hide the impatient look she aimed at Gisele. The coral-colored lips beneath the elegant coif and perfectly made-up face moved, forming words and sentences that washed over Gisele without meaning, lost amid the rush of blood against her eardrums.

"Take George's seat, Gisele," the boss repeated, gesturing to the chair on her right. "You're the new head of Casual Wear."

Still, Gisele could not move. The man beside George's seat stood and pulled the chair out for her. The woman next to him started clapping, others joining in. Gisele looked from face to face, seeing smiles and welcome. She couldn't speak.

Moving to George's chair, she sank into it, overwhelmed by a sense of wonder. The day had gone from deepest gloom to her brightest moment yet, and Gisele wanted to hold onto this golden feeling.

She was one of the team.

On the table in front of her rested a name plate, made from polished cherry wood, engraved in a handsome gold script: Gisele Ngono, Head Designer.

Gisele looked at Ms. Bonaventura. The woman smiled back at her. "I hope you'll call me Karen," she said. "Ms. Bonaventura takes too long to say. I'm paying you to design for me, not waste time over my long last name."

Gisele looked into the steel blue eyes—the eyes that had once frightened her—and saw compassion, humor, and a keen intelligence. Gratitude flooded over her, warm and splendid, feeling wonderful.

She thought of George, how he'd opened this door for her. A sudden painful twist wrung Gisele's heart and she wished he could be sitting there beside her. She would miss him so tremendously, but had to accept that he wasn't coming back.

He had opened the door and got her foot inside, and now Karen held the door wide, beckoning Gisele into a world of possibility.

It was up to her to dance.

*

Joslyn Chase is the author of the thriller, Nocturne In Ashes, an explosive read that will keep you turning pages to the end. What Leads A Man To Murder, her collection of short suspense, is available for free at joslynchase.com. Joslyn loves traveling, teaching, and playing the piano.

.

HUNGER
Justin Boote

Martin pounced when he saw the mouse scurrying through the snow. He grabbed it by the tail, twisted its neck and put it in his pocket. He started drooling almost immediately. This was tantamount to a three-course meal, surely enough to get him through another day without starving to death or looking at his dead friend back at the tent. Maybe it was a sign—a gift from God. He scoffed. If God existed, he wouldn't have left him to die on this godforsaken mountain in the first place. He wouldn't have let his best friend Jack die already.

Martin returned to the tent, his hands already numb, his toes distant relatives long forgotten. The wind sang its cruel tune, howling and crying, the depleted muscle tissue on Martin's body singing its own painful melody as it wasted away, desperately seeking nourishment from any available source. He figured that if help didn't come soon, he might waste away until there was nothing left of him—just bare bones for the local wildlife to feast upon. His ex-wife would have been proud. She had nagged him for years to reduce the beer gut that hung down over his trousers like a mutant growth, and here he was, he had finally achieved it without having to so much as glance at a gym or diet plan. He was living the ultimate diet.

Martin removed the mouse from his pocket and devoured it, leaving nothing to waste. He pulled the sleeping bag up tight against his chin and waited for the shivering to stop, praying that the incessant blizzard might finally ease up, too. It had been snowing and blowing a gale for so long now, he'd lost count. A week? Two? He knew the area was subject to bad weather, but this bad and for so long? This was the Scottish Highlands, not the Antarctic. People came up here to admire the view, spend the day enjoying the solitude of the place, then return home and act as though they'd climbed Everest. Not lie here starving to death and wondering with each new day if this was to be the last. And the last day was surely creeping up on him with each passing minute, like Death's stopwatch.

"How you doing, Jack? Warm enough where you are?" He laughed, then clamped a hand over his mouth to prevent himself from laughing harder. He found himself laughing uncontrollably more and more often as the days passed and the hunger ate at him like a cancerous predator. He cried a lot, too, but the lack of body tissue made his eyes sting when no tears ran. He couldn't even remember the last time he'd taken a leak.

"You think anyone'll find us, mate? Search party getting closer?" Occasionally he thought he really did hear dogs barking and his hope returned like a lost soul, only for it to fade away when the wind changed course. He had known from the beginning, since the blizzard started and Jack had slipped and cracked his head open, that the future looked doomed. It had been Jack's idea to be more adventurous, walk a little further, a little higher. Well, look at him now: no more adventures for him, unless he was standing at the crossroads between heaven and hell and unsure which direction to take. In a way, Martin envied him. He sure didn't care where his next meal was coming from now, did he? Or if they'd be rescued. In a way, he already had been.

Martin chuckled, pulling down hard on his earlobe to stop the hysterics from erupting again. He looked at Jack's stiff, cold body, thought of the mouse, and another thought ran through his mind. Maybe…surely anyone else would do the same? It was all about survival, doing what it takes. Up here no one was going to judge him. No one would call him a monster—a depraved, sick animal. They would congratulate him for having the courage, the will to survive. And really, Jack wasn't going anywhere, was he? Christ, no one even had to know.

"No. I can't. I can't do it. One more day. Surely someone will find me." He had to have hope, belief that someone would stumble upon them, see the tent and come running, but it was so hard. His stomach didn't even hurt him anymore, the grumbling, aching pains that kept him awake all night as he prayed for help. He promised he'd go to church every day, change his ways, donate half his earnings to charity. Just, please...help.

He closed his eyes after taking one more good look at Jack's half-frozen body, wondering, imagining. Desperate. With snow to hydrate with, as long as it melted first and wasn't so cold, he could survive another month if he was careful. The blizzard would eventually stop. No one would know...

Martin awoke some time the next day, unsure if he had slept minutes or hours; his body didn't feel anything anymore except that incessant gnawing at his muscle tissue. He looked to see that his skeletal hand was wrapped feebly around Jack's arm like when he tore a chicken wing from a plump Sunday roast. He wiped his mouth; he had been salivating, losing precious liquids. Disgusted, he pulled his hand away and edged further from Jack. Outside, the wind continued its monotonous, deafening howl, tearing at the tent just as he imagined tearing at the...

"No!" he cried, his throat like sandpaper, the force of his cry making him cough and splutter. He took out the flask that he kept inside his jacket filled with melted snow and sipped a little, picked up his phone as if it had magically charged overnight. He threw it away. A noise came from outside. A dog! That was a dog barking. Sobbing in relief, he climbed out of the tent and stood up, swaying with dizziness and the effort required. It came again. From straight ahead, then behind, then above. Miles above and all around.

Martin sank to the ground again. End it now, he told himself. Just throw yourself down the mountain, it would be quicker. No more hunger, no more hallucinations. And yet, there still remained a vestige of determination somewhere deep inside him, telling him to wait. Just a little longer. He told himself he would be saved, then spend a month doing the circuits on television, the interviews, the book. The money he would make.

He saw a dead mouse beneath the snow. He grabbed it and ate it. And then he thought about life expectancies. Would they really still be looking for him after all this time? Did they have the same hope within them that he desperately clung to? He didn't think so. He thought that hope was a very dangerous thing to have sometimes. Something that one grabbed with both hands as though a lifeline, and yet, could also blind one to reality. And the reality was that Martin was dying. It was hope that was making him suffer day after day when he could make it so easier for himself. End the suffering.

He climbed back in the tent and held his head in his hands. Looked at Jack. "This is all your damn fault. Why'd you have to take us higher? You knew it was dangerous. Or did you take us there on purpose? How often had you talked about suicide? Well, there, got what you wanted. But what about me?"

A faint tingling of adrenaline flickered through his body, the anger at what Jack had provoked causing his weak muscles to tense slightly. He had suggested coming up here to see things with a new perspective; alone, surrounded by nothing but mountains and views, figure a way of getting his life back together again after his wife left him. What was it he had said? "I've had enough, Martin. I can't carry on without her. Maybe I should end it all now?"

Had that been his plan, after all, the selfish pig? Kill himself and not give a damn about me?

"That's not fair, Jack. You left me to starve to death. How could you?"

Martin wiped his dry eyes and cuddled up to his blanket, but not before running a hand over Jack's arm again. Then, a thought occurred to him. Jack had been dead three days now. How long before decomposition occurred despite being almost frozen? He was too weak to drag him from the tent and the thought of watching him slowly decay and rot filled him with yet more horror. Would he, himself, die before the worms and bugs started on Jack? Would he have to sit and watch his best friend slowly eaten alive while he sat there starving to death?

"Well, at least I'll have plenty to eat then, won't I. I'm sure bugs are pretty tasty when one's starving to death," he said and drifted off into another restless sleep.

*

It was the sound of the wind screeching outside that woke him. It sounded more furious than ever. How was that possible? It barked and howled, whistling its terrible tale, the sound echoing off Martin's bones, stinging his heart. No one would be able to make the journey up here and find them. He wiped his mouth, the saliva or whatever it was leaving a dirty smear on his hand. His stomach ached again. This was strange. It had long since given up any attempts at communicating with him, merely withering away, leaving a nest of rotting intestines. He pushed himself to a sitting position. Once again, he could hear dogs barking outside, yet this time, he refused to fall for the trick. Nature and Death were taunting him, even as he lay here dying, beckoning him with false claims of survival.

Then, the wind tore open the tent, the entrance flapping wildly. He looked up.

"Hey, there's one here, still alive!"

A face peered in. "Hey, pal! Don't worry, you're safe. Rescue's here."

The words entered Martin's ears but his brain failed to respond, as though his brain had already given up, like the rest of him. All he could do was stare at the person before him and mumble something unintelligible. His despair increased. How could his brain trick him so? Wasn't it enough to have the wind mocking him? And then, he felt himself being dragged slowly from the tent, then lifted and laid back down, rapidly covered by a thick blanket.

"Let's get him down, quick. He doesn't look like he's got much left in him," he heard.

Martin looked up to see he was being taken away from the tent, floating in the air as four men carried him. Or were they really angels and he had died, after all, now being taken to the next stop?

"You're lucky, pal. We almost gave up hope. You can thank the dogs. Speaking of which, what the hell attacked your friend? Something made a mess of his arm. What's left of it, anyway. Looks like something tore a great chunk out of it."

Martin said nothing and allowed himself to fall into a long, deep sleep.

*

Justin Boote is an Englishman living in Barcelona for over 25 years and has been writing short horror stories for 3 years. In this time, he has published around 30 stories in diverse magazines and anthologies. He can be found at Facebook under his own name or his Amazon author page:
https://www.amazon.co.uk/Justin-Boote/e/B073Q44SZP

HOPE 2020
M.C. Dalton

On the television, when there was a funeral, it always rained.

But not in real life, not on the first day of the darkest days of Toby Mikkleson's life.

Mother-sun burned hard and hot, forcing the handful of grownups present to don their sunglasses and search for shade in the stark, dust-ridden cemetery. Her heat radiated and beat down on his head, mocking him with a fake happiness.

Six-year-old Toby stood alone beside the large hole that cradled the wooden box inside which his mother lay. Summer gusts sprinkled red sand on his well-worn trainers and up his nose. Tears painted streaks across his chubby little cheeks, and his heart howled with loneliness.

Behind him stood the lady who had brought him from the children's home. She was tall and cold. Cold like Mamma's hand when he'd held it that night. He remembered her eyes as their light faded, taking any hope of a good life with it.

Hope is a strange word. It's one which manifests both the notion of something good, like a pot of gold at the end of the rainbow, and something bad like the terrible disappointment when things simply don't go the way we'd... hoped.

Such was the indelible life lesson small Toby learned after the police dragged him screaming from the bloodied, limp body of his mother. Hope had deserted him; robbed his life of all her wonder and left him to fend for himself.

Mamma had always said that there could be no light in this world without Hope.

Hope was all he had. It was his fairy godmother on a stormy night, his warrior in the dark when things went bump, his ice cream after a bad day at school. Hope was all that was left of his mother. But Hope had deserted him and like his memories of Mamma, it faded into the mist of forgotten souls.

Today he was fifteen. No longer a child, no longer the lost little boy, and no longer the bigger boys' toy and punching bag. This morning he'd stood up to Thabo when the boy, a year older and three kids larger than he, had tried to dunk his head in the dirty toilet again.

He'd used every ounce of strength he owned and beat the fat bully who shared his foster home on number 15 Crescent Street, into a blubbering submission. He was also not going to stick around and wait for Thabo's cronies to dole out their payback. No, he was done with this life. It was up to him to make his own luck now.

Toby jumped the fence of the dilapidated old house. His threadbare trainers slapped the sidewalk with a gleeful sound. He'd lifted a few hundred Rand from his fat, smelly, foul-mouthed foster mother's purse and safely tucked them in a pocket he'd sewn into his hand-me-down undies for just such an occasion.

With bloodied knuckles, he adjusted his well-worn cap on top of his unruly mop of sun-drenched curls, tucked his baggy shirt into the pair of jeans he'd grabbed out of Masingo's drawer — it was the only piece of clothing which looked halfway new — and made a run for it.

No one had seen him.

He swung his small kit bag over his shoulder and trotted down the sidewalk toward the nearest bus stop. The bag held his most precious possessions: his only possessions. A teddy Mamma had bought him on his fourth birthday, a hat signed by cricket legend Jonty Rhodes, and a simple, cheap

GLIMMER

cricket bat he'd won in a school cricket tournament last year.

Cricket was his passion, arguably the only thing which made sense in his crazy, lonely life. This prestigious game, played in white, was his dream and his... no, not his hope, never hope, but it sure as heck was his companion and perhaps one day his meal ticket? He was good, on the verge of great. That was what his PE teacher had said.

Toby stopped running when he was far enough away. Across the street stood a rusted old bus stop. He didn't care where the bus went. All he cared was that it took him away, far away from the dingy, dank streets of Hillbrow. Away from the memory that he was a nobody, alone and worthless.

It was up to him, and him alone to make his life better. He wasn't sure how, but he would make his name in the world of cricket. He would succeed, but first he had to escape the darkness.

The 6:06 to Illovo pulled up and Toby reached into his back pocket for the nine-rand-sixty bus fare. Bus drivers hated giving change; only taxis used money anymore.

The round, Vaseline-smeared face of the middle-aged female driver considered him. For a moment, Toby feared she might point one of her sharp, long, blood-red fingernails in his face and call him a thief. But she didn't. Her plump brown cheeks bulged as she huffed, "Phakisa! Hurry up."

He dumped the exact amount into her cash register and took a seat in the middle row, at the window.

The doors closed with a sigh and the bus jolted forward when someone hammered on them. The driver chided, stopped and opened the doors, "Ke eng lihele! What the hell!" She leaned out of her seat then shook her head, "Damn Tsotsi's throwing stones again."

A young girl hopped up the steps, "No Tsotsi today Ma." She smiled and swiped her traveller's card. The driver took off before the doors closed properly, shaking her head as she muttered something to herself.

Toby couldn't help but stare. Walking toward him was

the most beautiful face he'd laid his eyes on, in forever. Her short, platinum pixie cut accentuated fine ears from which dangled a thousand silver rings and diamante studs. Her eyes a bright, bold green, and her lips as red as freshly picked strawberries.

"Can I sit here?" She pointed to the open seat beside him. All Toby could do was nod. She giggled, the sound like the flurry of an angel's wings wrapped around them, comforting him like Mamma's arms once had.

Her soft apricots-and-peaches scent warmed the hollow in his chest. And a funny tingle stirred in the centre of his being, but Toby pushed it away. Good things only happened to the special ones.

He turned his head and stared out the window.

"Where you off to?" She poked his shoulder like an older annoying sister would.

Toby looked to where her green gaze landed on his bag. *Great, a nosey parker.*

"Is that a cricket bat?" She reached forward but he moved it from her reach.

"Sorry." She held her hands up.

He squished his eyes shut and bit his bottom lip. Why was she asking so many questions? Couldn't she just play on her phone like all the other ignorant, self-absorbed humans on this bus? Perhaps she was from Children Services and was simply buddying up to him to grab him later and drag him back to the home!

"Well?" She pushed for an answer.

Toby readied himself to jump from the bus when it pulled up to the next stop. He shifted his body and then froze. Her name tag read *Hope.*

Seriously, Hope?

His eyes stumbled up and Toby found himself entranced by her malachite gaze.

"So you're on your way to Wanderers."

"How do you know?" Her statement struck him like one of Thabo's gut punches.

Illovo. That was where Wanderers' cricket stadium was situated and if memory served, it was where the junior cricket league tryouts were taking place. Today!

"Of course you are. A strapping young boy like you? I'm also heading out that way. I work at the kiosk. Got a part time possie there because of my bro. Dale McAvoy? Do you know him?" Excitement fluttered from her like a crisp spring gust.

Toby shook his head. He was dreaming!

This girl was like fairy dust on an overcast day. Toby clutched at his chest. In all his life, of all the bad turns and all the wrong people — now life decided to lead him to this point. To offer him a break on a silver tray, right here, now, where he sat beside the sister of THE. Dale. McAvoy., the Protea's best fast bowler since Alan Donald!

"Agh, I knew I shouldn't have said anything. People always go quiet and check me out with a crooked eye when I say that, but it's true, I swear, hand on the Bible." She raised her right hand sincerely.

Hope cocked her head and squinted her eyes. She pulled a Chubba Chubba out of her pocket, ripped off the wrapper and shoved the bright pink lollipop into her mouth.

"You weren't heading to Wanderers, were you?"

Panic surged through Toby's veins and froze in his lungs. Here it was then. This was it, just when he'd thought his luck had changed.

Hope smiled and offered him a Chubba Chubba, "Relax man. I'll get you in." She winked and shoved her Skull Candy on her head.

*

Toby stepped off the bus, his heart revved like a V8 engine without oil. In one hand, he held a Chubba Chubba, in the other, his kit bag. The bus had stopped in front of the magnificent stadium. His dream come true.

Toby watched as throngs of young boys and girls, clad

in their cricket bests, streamed through the well-advertised front entrance. Hope hopped off in front of him and ran through the gate, disappearing between all the excited bodies.

"Come on then!" Her white cropped head poked out from a small side gate.

Toby choked back his fear, gripped his Chubba Chubba and his kit bag and followed the platinum-haired pixie through the gate and into the stadium. Awe swallowed him whole as he took in the green pitch, the neatly trimmed lawn, the thousands of seats in the stands, and the practice nets. Even the air smelled different inside, like wood and sunscreen, leather and sweat.

"Come on, I don't have all day, you know." She waved to him, her smile brighter than ever.

Toby followed Hope and the pair made their way around the edge of the stadium to the cloakrooms. There were two parts to the large indoor player area. One where all the boys and girls found their separate change rooms and lockers to prepare for their day of intensive training with the best South Africa had to offer; the other — for the Proteas.

"Wait here." Hope put up a hand before she slipped into the players locker room. Toby wanted to warn her that perhaps it wasn't such a good idea. But maybe she'd done this before?

Moments turned into minutes as the black arms of the white-faced clock on the far side of the passage shifted. Doubt rose like the incoming tide of a hungry ocean. His hand tightened around the straps of his kitbag, the other lifted the Chubba Chubba to his face. What was he doing here? Sweat trickled down his temple and neck. Fear pooled in the pit of his stomach before it pushed up his gullet.

How silly he was to follow some girl off a bus and into Wanderers. Hope was obviously pulling his leg. She was probably sitting inside, laughing her head off with all the players, as they joked about the poor little orphan waiting outside.

Why would anything good ever happen to him? He was a nobody. An orphan who Thabo had made clear was worth nothing more than a *bliksem* bag. Everything that had been good in his life was buried in that casket in the Brixton Cemetery.

His feet shuffled this way and that as his eyes searched for a way out. He had to leave before someone found him and dragged him back to that house. Toby spun full circle on the spot, the walls closed in, and his lungs cramped as they strained for air. His muscles tensed and blood drained from his head, painting black spots across his vision.

Voices exiting the Protea's cloakrooms grabbed his attention. Toby swung around and took off, running straight into a tall, solid body.

"Ompf!"

His lollipop went flying in one direction and his kit bag in the other.

"Sorry Sir…"

"Hey, young man…"

Toby looked up into the grass-green eyes of Dale McAvoy. His legs turned to mush and he sat flat on his bum.

"You okay there, my boy?" The tall, fair haired, fast bowler stretched out a hand.

"Ah, yes, I ah…Where's Hope?"

South Africa's number one fast bowler retracted his hand and frowned, his gaze darkened. "Are you kidding me?"

"No Sir. I met her on the bus and she said…."

Dale wiped a hand over his face, then looked to the side. He knelt and picked up the Chubba Chubba, "This yours?"

Toby nodded. "She gave it to me."

He held out his hand and Dale dropped the lollipop in it before Toby hugged it possessively to his chest.

The cricket player sat on the floor beside him, smiling at the un-opened lollipop.

"It was her favourite. You catch the 6:06 from Hillbrow to Illovo?"

"Uh, yes." Toby searched for an exit as he stood. Something was odd. He needed a way to make a quick escape before any authorities were called.

"Do you have a minute?" Dale dusted himself off as he stood.

Toby stepped back, looking this way and that.

"You're not in trouble."

He looked up as Dale blinked away a tear.

"Look, it's a long story…"

"Okay." He would give the bloke a chance to explain. He didn't know why, but perhaps it was some of that pixie dust Hope was sprinkling around?

"Where is Hope?" he asked again.

"This way," Dale took Toby upstairs to the players' lounge where he offered him a Coke, "I am sorry. But Hope…well she…it's five years today."

Toby froze, soda can in mid-air. Hope was dead? He slumped back into his chair. That explained a lot. Only a ghost, a figment of his imagination could be that kind to the likes of him. He'd sent out a desperate plea when Thabo had beat him up for the umpteenth time and Hope had answered. But how would a ghost help him any?

"I was six when Mamma died." He didn't know what else to say.

A sad smile slid across the cricket player's face, "She found you on the bus?"

Toby nodded.

"She lived for those who were lost. She believed she was Wonder Woman. Always out to save the world and all those in it. That's what cost her, her life," Dale stood and stared out over the field dotted with excited young players.

*

"Mamma always said there'd be no light in the world without Hope."

Toby Mikkelson stood at the podium. In his hands was

the plaque for Sportsman of the Year.

"I dedicate this plaque to my best friend and his sister, Hope. You who took a chance on me when many wouldn't. You reminded me, no matter how dark the days may get, Hope never abandons us."

Toby thanked his audience and fellow players before returning to his table. His wife, with her swollen belly smiling proudly up at him. Beside her, his best bud, Dale McAvoy.

*

Originally from Pretoria, South Africa, Michelle Dalton and her family fled the rising violence taking over her beloved country and now lives near Brisbane, Australia with her husband and triplet sons.

While also juggling a nursing career and teenage sons, she loves to escape into her fictional world. Michelle has a deep love of horses and enjoys weaving them into dramatic stories with honourable men and strong women.

Her other hobbies are gardening (usually trying to save her precious herbs and bulbs from an overactive miniature Jack Russell), painting, and reading. She's also a huge Star Trek and Marvel Comics fan, and as of recently a wee fan of DC too.

https://michelledaltonauthor.com

SILENCE
Gary Little

Albert Cyrano Walton was about to have the worst day of his life.

"Con, Chief Petty Officer Walton," he called through his suit's communication system.

"Con," the Control Room replied.

"Exiting, starboard lock number two."

"Roger. Logged. Where ya going so early, AC?"

"Inspecting the starboard pylon."

"Roger. Exit confirmed."

This was the four hundred and third day of the pioneering voyage of the United Star Ship Goddard-Lemaître, or as the crew called her, the Goodship Lollipop. Why those two historical figures? Goddard because of the beginning of rocketry. Lemaître because of cosmology. The real reason? No one had ever named a ship Goddard or Lemaître. There would be no confusion, no wondering which one, Teddy or Franklin. The Goddard-Lemaître was the first ship of its class, the first starship built by humanity, and the first ship with that name.

But, it had not been finished and they had left a wee bit early from Lunar Orbital Dock. Last night during midwatch, someone complained about a bumping sound coming from the starboard pylon. The captain ordered the Lollipop out of hyperspace to inspect the pylon and AC had drawn the duty.

He mumbled not-so-nice expletives about someone and

GLIMMER

their bumps in the night as he pulled on his Engineering EVA suit.

"God damn XO, that's who was doing the grumbling. Nothing wrong with that pylon. I inspected it two days ago." On and on he continued the grumble, but only to himself, and with the VOX set to Push-to-talk.

He pressed the Cycle button and heard the faint whisper of pressure being bled from the airlock. Changing pressure plugged his ears and he cleared them. When cycling finished, he checked his tether, and then pressed the Big Red exit button.

"Con, Walton, door opening."

"Roger ... uh ... hold on Chief."

Walton grabbed the handle next to the hatch to pull himself out but stopped at the last command from the Control Room.

"Got a problem?" he said.

"We're showing activity on the starboard side ... "

Undefined noises followed and someone said, "what ... hell ..."

Walton heard a pop, a bang, what sounded like a scream and then silence. The lights in the lock went out and he was deep in the dark of interstellar space.

"Con, Walton, over. Talk to me, Bobbie."

Through the open hatch, he saw the stars begin to rotate and he impacted the inner wall of the airlock.

"What the hell?" Spin was supposed to be off the ship until after he finished his inspection. The stars should not be moving.

AC pushed the hatch close button. Nothing. Power out. He engaged his mag boots, reached out, and up to manually shut the hatch and looked forward. He froze. There was a cloud of debris where the Control Room and Bridge should have been. The debris appeared to have a familiar kind of swirl and dance to it.

Without warning the hatch swung away, trapping his right gauntlet. He struggled to free his arm and then he was flung away as the hatch and ship rotated away. He tumbled end over end with a very nasty twist until he came to the end of the tether. All that tumble and twist had wrapped the tether around his suit a couple of times, one loop passing over a shoulder, down his chest, and back between his legs.

At the end of the tether, spinning like a yoyo, he came to the over-the-shoulder and between the legs loop. Like a bullwhip, he snapped forward and doubled up like a taco. He thought he heard a "twang" when the tether snapped taut.

AC took stock of the situation as his head stopped swimming. His nose hurt, and he tasted the saltiness of blood. His forehead stung, and he figured the hide had been knocked off when his face impacted his helmet. He scanned suit status in the heads up display. The suit was sound, still airtight and functional, and medical repeated what he knew. He might be a little banged up, but he was still in one piece.

He was rotating to face the ship and what he saw did not inspire joy.

The Lollipop was in trouble. His only source of life support for at least a hundred and fifty light-years looked like it was … eating itself. He watched bulkhead after bulkhead collapse inwards and join an ever-growing whirl of a glowing disk.

He hit the tether disconnect. Nothing. His bullwhip snap at the end must have jammed it.

"Damn … damn …" became a mantra as he tried everything to free the tether. He had no chance if he fell into that ever-growing maelstrom where the Bridge used to be.

"Damn … damn …" he grabbed his belt knife and swung at the tether. It hit, but he needed tension to cut. He took a bite in the tether with his left hand, wrapped it under his left elbow, and tried the knife again. It slipped. He and the tether struggled but the diamond edge of the suit knife found purchase and severed the snake dragging him to his doom. He snapped the knife back to his belt.

Momentum from the snapback still carried him where

he did not want to go. The ship. AC estimated 15 minutes, max, before the Cargo Deck, Starboard #2 Lock was consumed by ... what? A glowing disk of debris that looked like a ...

Somewhere, some time in one of his classes, he had seen this: an accretion disk. The shape of matter swirling inwards and heating up as it fell into a black hole or a protostar. But where did a protostar come from? The ship's computer should have detected it and navigated around it. Their route skirted all known black holes, protostars, or singularities ...

"Oh, crap ..."

Except for the singularity in the Engine Room. Their source of power and propulsion.

The containment field could not fail, the whiz-kids had assured them, but they had spent a lot of time going over procedures in case it did. He remembered one graphic; a ship being consumed from the middle out.

"Great, great, just f'ing great," he said to the universe.

He took a moment to think. "Suit thrusters won't get me away. Not by themselves," he muttered, oriented himself, and hit max thrust. His course took him not away, but towards what he hoped was a clear area close to the accretion disk. He was trying for what he had seen many times in fictional cinema. He had even heard of it used by several pilots. A slingshot. A path that would bring him closer to the singularity than he wanted, but just might give him enough speed on the other side to throw him clear of the destruction of the ship.

The idea was sound. That singularity had enough mass, but was smaller than the dot of the lowercase letter "i". It had the mass of a 250-kilometer nickel-iron asteroid. His plan might work.

If he survived passing that close to a singularity.

If there wasn't a piece of debris with his name on it.

A thousand if's but only one chance.

Max thrust. He had never been in an engineering suit using max thrust and now he knew why. He felt like his crotch was being bifurcated by the groin of the suit.

He bit his lower lip and verbally voiced his opinion of his decision. Several times. At last, the thrust sputtered and inertia pushed him back into the helmet. Thrust ended and he either sped to a quick death, or it would work and he would be thrown away, or he would orbit back around to spiral in any way. Gauntleted hands went to his crotch and he tried to comfort what had been abused. Difficult through several layers of suit and glove, but it was the thought that counted.

He watched the now glowing realm of destruction approach with a macabre fascination. He could not look away. Ripped into ever smaller pieces, debris continued to feed the monster.

He wondered about the Hole Gang he worked with in Engineering. That would have been the first to go once the containment field breached. It was where AC would have been, had he not been inspecting the starboard pylon.

"I hope it was quick."

He continued his trajectory towards a spot he hoped would not be too close and not be too far. He needed it to be just right. He checked the path in his heads up display and began to worry.

He was making a noticeable arc a bit further inward than he wanted. The monster's invisible warping of time and space was already affecting him. He watched the illustrated line of his projected path in his heads-up display bend ever so slightly towards the singularity.

His thrusters had no fuel. All he could control was his attitude; which way he faced.

His emotional attitude was another thing. That was one of a mouse, the one flipping off the cat. A final act of defiance.

He began to feel the effects of all that warping of space-time that was destroying his ship. He was yawing, rotating to starboard, and he decided he wanted to go into the maelstrom feet first. That he could control.

GLIMMER

AC spread his feet apart and had an incredible view. No one, to his knowledge, had ever gotten this close to an event horizon. It was a bit difficult to get in and out of such a place with your hide, let alone any data you may have gathered. AC had a front-row seat to something no human had ever seen.

There were disturbances here and there in that glowing all-consuming mouth. Maybe a tank or two of gas collapsed, its contents outgassing all at once added to the heat and turmoil.

At his closest approach, AC could feel himself being pulled feet first into the monster's maw. Like going to the max with his thrusters, his crotch was again becoming too intimate with the groin of his suit.

He passed perigee, and he was still alive. The spaghettifying forces eased, but he did not celebrate. His fascination was complete, watching his ship crinkle and collapse into that hole in space.

He re-oriented his suit to face the torrent instead of trying to look between his booted feet and watched the target of his inspection bend 90 degrees and the entire pylon fold down into the maelstrom. It was like watching a tornado back home in Kansas hit a barn and tear it apart, the barn adding bits and pieces to the whirling cloud of debris.

He watched forty thousand metric tonnes of adamantine steel, glass, diamond sheeting, and plastic, gone. A crew of twelve hundred gone. Earth's first interstellar ship, gone. Earth's best and brightest people, gone. All his life support and yeah, even the mess hall's chipped beef on toast. Gone.

He looked at his chronometer. Thirteen minutes since he had closed his helmet and started the timer. All gone in thirteen minutes.

Checking his orbital path he confirmed his trajectory. He was not on a parabolic path. He would loop around and fall into that newly created black hole in about thirty-two hours. And there was not one thing he could do about it. So ... he watched. He watched all that debris spin into the invisible something at the center. He watched the glow from the friction as materials collided with each other, becoming brighter and brighter.

Hours later, but still a long time from his own encounter, he noted the accretion disk getting smaller and dimmer. Less and less material fell into the singularity. Six hours away, he witnessed the glow dim, flicker, and cease. It was no longer feeding. The show was over.

"Now what?" AC wondered. "It sits there and just digests its dinner until it gets me for dessert?"

He continued to watch and sixty minutes later AC witnessed a single, incredibly bright flash. He swore he heard a pfft!

What the ... he thought. He checked his course. It was no longer a spiral, but that was impossible. Mass just did not disappear. AC checked it again. It was correct. He would continue this direction until he hit something, or something hit him, but it would not be the singularity.

How in the hell could that happen?

The answer came when he checked the database in his suit. He found it. The singularity that powered the Goodship Lollipop was designed to evaporate soon after it finished feeding. Engineering kept a critical eye on the mass the singularity was consuming and fed it just a trickle compared to the forty-thousand-ton ship it had just consumed. That trickle could last for decades, and consist of a mass orders of magnitude greater than the Lollipop.

He played it over in his mind. The containment field had collapsed. Why? AC did not know. That impossibly hungry spot in spacetime began to feed on anything and everything near it until, like its larger brothers, there was nothing left to eat. Then it did what it had been designed to do. It ... evaporated.

AC stared at the spot that had so diligently consumed all his friends, all his food, all his oxygen, every last little bit of his only means to get anywhere. He turned to face where

GLIMMER

the destination had been some twenty hours ago, there in that constellation of Orion. Lightyears away. Tens of millions of years away.

He depressed the push to talk button and said, "Con, Walton, over."

Silence.

"Anybody? Walton, over."

He released the push-to-talk button and watched those motionless stars.

"Great, great, just f'ing great," and in defiance, he raised a middle finger.

*

Gary Little has been stringing letters into words for seven decades. From sermons, for a very short time, to forty years of writing low-level system software for computers, to finally writing what he wants to write. Widowed and living in Las Vegas, Gary manages to knock out short stories and irreverent gedankens on an irregular schedule.

LONG RANGE TRANSMISSION
Sef Churchill

Mrs Jones Next Door started the trouble by telling half the street she could hear Mum entertaining Men. She betrayed us over the garden fence, and I heard her, loud and clear.

"Last thing at night," said Mrs JND to her neighbour on the far side, Mrs Parks.

I stood in our garden behind the sheets I was pegging out for Mum. They were long, flannel sheets, heavy although they'd been through the wringer, and they hid me perfectly. I peeped between wet ghosts to see the conversation.

Mrs JND added, "Not just one man either. From the way she talks to them, there's lots."

There was a pause as the grind of a plane's engines grew nearer, and we all looked up, habitually making sure it was one of ours. It was – a Hurricane. We waited as it scraped across the sky and disappeared towards the coast. Then, "All at once?" said Mrs Parks.

Mrs JND nodded grimly. "And her with Little Ann in the house too."

I grimaced at my nickname, but even Mum called me that although I was eleven. It's because her name was Ann Spratt too, same as me. It was Dad's habit, and you can't complain about a dead person. It is not allowed, for various reasons.

The wind sent a bloom of November air under the washing, and the sheets lifted and fell like sad flags.

GLIMMER.

The women noticed me then, standing with the stick from a lollipop in my mouth like Mum's cigarette.

"Oi," said Mrs JND. "Seen and not heard!"

I had to smile because that's exactly what I was.

"I mean hop it," she said and jerked her thumb towards our back door.

I hopped it, into the warm kitchen full of steam and soap-smell.

"Mum," I said, "Mrs JND is at it again.".

Mum stood at the big square sink, her arms up to the elbows in suds, her face pink from scrubbing dirty smalls in boiling water. Her hair still shone, though, and under her practical apron she wore her favourite dress, the one swirled with green and blue sea-patterns. Nobody else's mum dressed like mine did. "What love?"

"She told Mrs Parks on the other side about you having visitors."

Mum's mouth hardened. Then she sighed, and her face cleared again. "That cow," she said calmly. "Well, not to worry, lovey. Words can't hurt us."

"It's not the words," I said, for I was a literal child. "She says she's heard you talking to lots of men at once. At night."

Mum withdrew her soapy hands from the washing's embrace and gripped me by the shoulders. "It's nothing," she said. "There are no visitors, all right? She's imagining it."

"I do hear you sometimes," I said. "Talking."

"Sometimes I can't sleep, love. I put the wireless on."

I bit my lip. What I heard was no wireless, but Mum would never say it. "It's loud sometimes," I said. "I mean your voice, it's loud." A slip — it was men's voices I heard, but Mum couldn't know that.

She let go of me and snatched up a tea-towel. She rubbed her hands clean, then absent-mindedly dabbed at the great damp patched on the shoulders of my cardigan. "Well," she said. "Well, then I'd better turn the sound down a bit. That

41

wireless is a bit ropey, you know."

Ropey? The wireless carried mainly a rush of static, and the occasional nasal voice reading out news from the war. I said nothing, though – Mum was tired, and I was hungry.

I glanced at Dad's place at the table, his chair, his cup and plate. They were in shadow, and if I squinted I could picture him, sitting silent, reading his paper.

In the hall the clock chimed. Apart from the wireless it was the only expensive thing we had. After Dad was killed Mum had sold the sideboard, and the wardrobe from the spare room and then the piano and the chairs, all but the ones in the front room. The front room looked much as it did before, before Dad went off in his lovely green uniform with his ugly kit bag and a snapshot in his pocket of us all eating ice-creams at Margate.

Where was that snapshot now? Buried in French mud? Sodden and black, its smiling faces all ruined? I would never see it again, that moment.

"It's three," I said. "They'll be here soon. You should get changed."

Mum untied her apron. "I don't give a fig for what they think of me."

"You get changed for-" I nearly said, the other visitors, but caught myself. "The evening."

"That's different," said Mum. "You go upstairs now. Read your book."

"Can I listen to the wireless in the front room?"

She hesitated. "I should sell that thing. The rent's due."

"I'll do the dusting at the same time."

Mum shook her head and smiled. "Go on then. But don't break anything!"

*

The visitors were women from the Institute, come to give Mum work. She couldn't join the land girls or the munitions factory, because she had me. Shop work in town was not considered suitable for a married woman, even a widowed one. So the Institute women brought Mum work - bits of laundry to do, and mending. Mum hated every minute of it – it was charity, dressed up as work – and I wished she would give it up.

The clock chimed four and I turned down the wireless. The women were leaving.

"We'll see you in the shelter later?" said Mrs Lyle, the chairwoman of the Institute.

"Probably," said Mum in the breezy tone that meant No.

I peeped through the crack in the parlour door. Mrs Lyle was formidable in a blue coat and hat, and a big brown handbag. Her shoes looked like axes. But she touched Mum's arm, not unkindly, and said, "It's not safe, dear. Think of your girl!"

"We've got the Anderson," said Mum stiffly. "We're fine."

"That won't survive a direct hit," said Mrs Lyle gently.

"Neither will the shelter," said Mum. "One bomb on a snowy Thursday night and they'll be digging you out for three days."

Something in the way she said it, as if it had already happened and she'd read it in the papers like just another sad story, made the Institute women shrink back. There was a little pause, and I heard the clock tick, tick, tick.

Then Mrs Lyle spoke and it was not so nicely. "Unless there's some other reason keeping you here," she said. "Some business you attend to at night."

"And what might that be?" said Mum frostily.

"I'm sure I don't know," said Mrs Lyle.

She and Mum stared at each other. The second woman shuffled her feet and clutched her handbag.

Behind me on the mantel, the wireless programme finished. Cheery music played and a plummy man announced weather and the news coming shortly. His voice was cut with static – we were a long way from the radio mast, and nothing came through very clear.

43

Mrs Lyle glanced in my direction. I retreated from the parlour door.

"Gentlemen callers," said Mrs Lyle in a low voice as if even the mention of it would taint her. "Gentleman callers at night, Ann. Mabel Jones said so. It's not right."

"There are no gentleman callers," Mum said angrily. "When has she ever seen any?"

"She hears you talking to them. Thin walls, you know."

"It's plays on the wireless. I have it on it at night to help me sleep."

"So far from the mast? Come on, Ann. I know you're short of money. I want to help. Before you start something desperate. You've Little Ann to think of."

"I do not want your pity," said Mum. It came out in a squeak of anger. "Please leave."

"The landlord won't stand for lewd behaviour," said Mrs Lyle. "Or late rent."

"I can pay my rent. I always have."

"It was due last Tuesday," she said. "I spoke to him myself."

I was shocked. Mum had never said we'd missed rent. Were we going to starve like the little foreign children in hot countries? I thought of their thin faces in the Sunday School newspaper, and swallowed.

"Please go," said Mum through gritted teeth.

"They'll take Little Ann to a Home," said Mrs Lyle. "Without a second thought. It only takes a word from a worried neighbour."

I peeped again. What would Mum say to this? Surely she would scoff at such an obvious lie!

Mum leaned back on the stair post suddenly and looked tired. "You're right," she muttered. "I'm sorry. My manners... what was I thinking when you've been so kind?" She lifted her gaze to them and a calm drifted over the hallway.

Mrs Lyle looked mollified. "You're a good girl at heart Ann. I don't want to see you falling into bad ways."

"Of course," said Mum. She summoned her smile, her dazzling sweet smile like a film star, and Mrs Lyle smiled too. "Same time next week then," said Mum and off went Mrs Lyle, perfectly happy.

The door shut with a click and Mum turned the key. "Come out," she said to me.

I crept into the hall.

"Take no notice of her," Mum said. "She's trying to frighten us, that's all."

"Maybe we should go to the shelter tonight," I said. "Show our faces?"

Mum sighed. "I can't love. If I'm not here-" She broke off. "Never mind all that. I've got to get ready. Make us a cup of tea, would you?"

Mrs Lyle's words frightened me more than any voices in the night. I watched and noticed from then on – how little Mum ate at tea-time. How she made her cup of tea last all evening. She'd given up sugar, even smoking. Mrs Lyle was right.

We were poor.

*

When the siren went off Mum shooed me under the kitchen table with my coat on and a slice of bread and butter. "Lights off," she said, flipping the switch. "Everything off and they'll pass over us in a jiffy."

We sat listening to the howl of the warning siren. Voices and hurrying footsteps passed our front door – heading for the big shelter.

When all was quiet again Mum crawled out. She checked her lipstick in the back of the frying pan. "Right then. You stay there, I'll be in the front room."

As the first bombs fell, far away on the other side of town, I heard the visitors arrive.

*

The veil is thinner at night, everyone knows that, and thinner still in winter. That winter, as the country was pummelled by enemy bombs and goaded with food shortages and fuel rations, it was as if there was no veil at all. The blackouts seemed to bring them, hungry and mournful, to crowd our front room and clamour for attention, attention Mum gave them because she had the gift, and a kind heart.

I couldn't bear to be left alone in the kitchen with planes burbling low over the roof and flashes and bangs going off in the crack under the blackout curtain. I slipped into the front room and sat down cross-legged behind the settee. A lamp was burning, turned down low, and set in the hearth so its yellow glow would not reach the windows.

Mum opened her eyes as I entered, and gave me a look, but continued her work.

She sat at the table, its shining oak covered with a heavy red cloth. Her hair was done and her lipstick perfect, and in front of her lay a spread of playing cards, although they were not the kind you use for Rummy. "One at a time, please," she said. She shook her head. "Quietly! I can't tell who is who like this."

I watched shamelessly, because she had her eyes closed and she couldn't see them, or me.

This lot were soldiers, as they so often were – men in uniform, mostly uniform like Dad's, but one or two in red coats, tall hats and tattered cockades like prize-winning rosettes. They filled the room and beyond – new bright ones beside Mum, jostling for her attention; old, dimmer ones at the back, smaller and more distant.

"Can you hear me?" said one. His face was gone and his uniform a mess of black. The Royal Air Force emblem hung, scorched, from one shoulder. "Is this real?"

"Yes! said Mum. "Tell me your name."

"Jim Peters."

"John – sorry, say again."

"Jim Peters."

"Jim Peters." She nodded. "Right then. Tell me your story-"

A bang exploded close by, and white light flashed through the room.

All the visitors flickered and faded, and then came back. When Jim Peters spoke, his voice was faint.

"I can't hear," said Mum.

The others began to press forward, elbowing each other insubstantially to get closer to Mum.

"Oi." She held up one of the cards and they recoiled. "One at a time!"

It went on like that, then, with Mum trying to hear them, to comfort them, and them shimmering in and out of the yellow lamplight, and bangs going off outside.

"Mum," I said as the explosions grew closer. The soldiers were shouting now, in shattered voices. "Mum!"

"What love?" She opened her eyes. She looked so tired. But I knew she wouldn't sleep until she'd spoken with every one that came.

I hesitated.

The men pressed near to me now in sorrowful desperation. I flinched, although they couldn't hurt me. Their misery dragged at me – they had lost their warmth, their life, their hope.

"Ann. You should be under the table."

"So should you! Why are you doing this?"

"Doing what?" said Mum in a different tone, and I remembered she was not supposed to know I knew.

*

The enemy was bombing the munitions factory on the other side of town. Aiming for it, anyway, and every crump I heard was a try, a miss of the works and a hit on someone's house or shop. The fire engine had been past twice, its bell jangling in the dark.

"I can hear them," I said to Mum. "The visitors."

Mum did not try to tell me that she talked to herself, or to the wireless. "What can you hear?"

"The men," I said. "The soldiers."

She drew a long breath and let it out even longer. The cards fluttered on the tablecloth. "You have the gift," she murmured. "No surprise, but you're so young!"

"I can see them too," I said, given I was confessing. "You should get them to hold up their identity cards so I can write down their names and numbers."

Mum gawped at me. "You see them."

"What's left of them," I said, aiming for her blithe film star voice, because now she knew I was just like her.

She made a face at me. "But clearly. Clearly enough to read their names?"

"Oh yes. Though that one-" I pointed at the Waterloo soldier –"is older, so he's not as bright."

Mum stared at me for a long time. The men shuffled and shouted, but she ignored them. "Right," she said at last. "Right."

She glanced over her shoulder at Dad's chair.

I looked too, and smiled.

"What do you do," I said, "with all this talking to them?"

She looked startled. "Comfort them, of course. Listen to their stories. That's why we have the gift. To pass messages across the veil."

I thought about this. Sunday school taught that the veil was impassable, sacred, fixed. Then they sent the plate round.

I said, "For nothing?"

Mum's mouth dropped open.

"They can't pay you," I said. "But their widows can. It would give them hope. And their children. I bet their children would love to hear from their fathers."

She gave me a sharp look then, and I saw that she understood, now. I shrugged. She had never been playing that wireless for comfort. The man's voice, late at night –

that came from somewhere much further away.

"If I can find out their addresses, we can write to them," I said. "Or maybe ... you can bring the women here. I'll speak to their husbands."

"We could say it was a bit of fortune telling, harmless fun," said Mum. "Just some mothers having tea. Bit of a morale boost."

I grinned. Around me, the soldiers had stilled, their heads tilted, their wounds dimmed as they listened to our conversation. They seemed brighter now, brighter and calmer as Mum spoke of tea. "Tea and comfort."

*

Mrs JND gave me a sour look as I took in the washing the next day. "It'll be ruined," she warned. She gestured at the ash, falling slowly through the winter air all around. "Your poor mother will have to do it all again!"

"My mother isn't poor," I said.

Mrs JND shook her head sadly at me. "The mouth on her! I suppose this is what happens. No father. Your mother will be missing your father in the house."

I smiled at that, and hugged the wet washing closer. "Oh no," I said. "We don't miss Dad at all."

*

Sef Churchill is a lifelong writer from the UK. She won a national writing award at age sixteen and promptly did nothing about it. Nowadays, she writes poetry and micro fiction and is active in several online writing communities. On http://sefchurchill.com, she offers wry creative guidance. Her book, Dread, is available to buy online.

WHO WANTS TO GO FOR A WALK?
Iseult Murphy

Katie lay on her back staring at the mould spots that freckled the ceiling above her bed. Her tablet dinged on her bedside locker, but she couldn't move to read the message. A heavy weight pressed down upon her body, forcing her limbs into the bare mattress and constricting her lungs.

It ends today.

She held onto that thought tightly.

By midmorning she could move sufficiently to roll onto her side and lever her body into a sitting position on the edge of the bed. She checked the time on her tablet. Eleven fifty-five. She saw the message icon blinking in the corner of the screen, so she pushed it with her finger.

You have received a notification from the National Health Board. Thank you for your application. You have been approved for treatment.

How long had she been waiting for help? Two years at least. It had arrived too little, too late. At least she would free up a space on the waiting list for someone else.

She pulled on her outdoor clothes. No need to wash when the river would soon claim her. Shoes and jacket were still necessary, but her wallet and keys could remain in the apartment.

The wind bit into her face as she walked down the steps of the tower block, buffeting her against the cold metal railing and generally reminded her of how unwelcome she was in the world.

She wouldn't be in it for much longer now.

A group of celebs congregated at the bottom of the stairs, men and women who had altered and augmented their bodies so that they all looked like their favourite famous person. Katie didn't recognise the pale skinned, black haired creature they emulated.

"Watch out, indy coming through."

Katie didn't understand why being called an individual was considered such a slur. She wore her original face like a badge of honour, resisted the addons and upgrades that made connection to the hive mind easier.

"Careful, Sandy, don't touch it, it might be catching."

The celebs cackled in unison. Katie shoved her hands deeper into her pockets and kept her head down as she walked past the group.

"Ouch, uggo burns my eyes. How can it bear to live?"

"Do us all a favour and die already, indy. Your kind should be extinct anyway."

Katie clenched her jaw. Part of her hated that she was about to do exactly what they wanted, but she wouldn't change her plans just to be contrary.

They continued to heckle her as she left the apartment complex and joined the walkway along the river. The Boyle surged brown and angry with flood waters, forcing the ducks and swans to shelter on the steep banks. Katie could climb over the railing here and jump, but she most likely would break something rolling down the embankment and she didn't relish the thought of floundering in the raging river. She wanted to end the pain of life, not make it worse.

The pedestrian bridge crossing the Boyle was her chosen spot. Spanning the broad river and practically deserted at this time of the day, its midpoint provided a high dive into oblivion. Yes, the ever-present hive would observe her, but without implants to keep her constantly plugged in, it would have to rely on old school face recognition and identity search, which should buy her enough time to complete her jump before authorities arrived to check her permits.

Bitter wind cut into her, freezing her already numb core, as she battled her way to the centre of the bridge. Spray from the water below cut into her cheeks and hid her tears. She gripped the metal railing with her bare hands and gazed up at the storm cloud covered sky.

This was it. Her very last moments. About to depart alone, unloved and uncared for, as she had been for the last two and a half decades. She searched the clouds for a chink of sunlight, but the gunmetal grey shield was unbroken.

In her periphery she saw figures approaching the bridge from the pathway on the bank. She had to move now, in case they happened to be a rare good Samaritan and tried to stop her rather than help push her in.

She climbed awkwardly onto the railing, forced to straddle it as its rounded edge made her plans for a stately standing dive too difficult. Perhaps an inelegant belly flop would be a more fitting full stop on her life anyway.

Closing her eyes and taking a final deep breathe, she let go of the railing and let gravity pull her towards the river.

Searing pain shot through her left ankle all the way up to her hip as her fall was arrested. She crashed into the parapet, bruising her ribs.

"Hey!"

She looked up and saw a large dog leaning over the railings of the bridge, holding her ankle tightly in a pair of little hands, like those of a racoon or a child, and its square jaws clamped onto her trousers, holding her back.

"Let go! Leave it! Bad dog!" Katie tried to shake the dog loose.

Her gyrations pulled the dog further over the railing and she caught sight of unusually large hind paws, so broad and flat they looked more like snowshoes than feet, flapping wildly at the railing supports to get purchase.

"Stop struggling, I'm trying to save you."

The dog's voice was growly, made worse by having to speak through a mouthful of fabric.

An augmented animal. Katie disliked them even more

than the humans. At least people could choose whether they destroyed their natural form, but animals that had been genetically altered and further cosmetically and mentally enhanced had no say in the matter. They were basically slaves. It was wrong.

"I don't want to be saved. It's none of your business."

She kicked at the dog, hitting its heavily furred chest with her right heel. The movement sent them both jolting downward as the dog was pulled further over the railing.

"Actually, it is, and stop kicking me or we'll both end up in the river. Did it occur to you that I don't want to die?"

Katie felt the dog's creepy little hands climbing up her leg and grabbing her more firmly. Her trousers slowly ripped as the dog, showing extreme strength, pulled her kicking and screaming over the railing and deposited her onto the trembling concrete of the bridge.

"Why did you do that?" She couldn't blame her tears on the weather any longer. They squeezed painfully out of her eyes, snot gathering at the back of her nose and drippling out one nostril.

The dog lay panting beside her, one hand resting on Katie's leg. "It's my job. I'm Sally, your therapy canine. When I couldn't find you in your apartment, I had to track your scent. I'd have found you quicker if you'd been part of the hive."

Katie choked on a snort. She winced at the pain in her ribs as she propped her back against the railings. Her trousers had ripped above the knee, but were still decent, even if the tear let the cold air into her skin. She rubbed her hip, trying to ease the pain from the jolt of Sally grabbing her.

"You must have known I was due today. Didn't you get the message that your application had been successful?"

"It's too late for me, go help someone else."

Sally looked away. "I've been engineered to your specifications. If you refuse treatment, I'll be scrapped. Now, tell me, why do you want to die?"

Katie looked more closely at the dog. No wonder the waiting time was so long. She hadn't known that each therapy was tailored to the patient. Sally looked almost as tall as her sitting on the bridge, but much bulkier because of her golden fur, accented with sable around her face, with a white ruff, chest and paws. Her long muzzle seemed odd, squashed into a boxy shape to accommodate altered tongue, teeth and lips that allowed human speech. Her eyes were likewise disturbingly human and expressive.

"I don't want to die exactly. I just want the pain to end."

"There's no guarantee things will be better in death you know."

"Thanks, but I don't believe in an afterlife."

The dog's hand squeezed her leg. "You prefer ceasing to exist rather than living with a bit of suffering?"

She pulled away from the dog. Sally didn't understand. How could she?

"I've tried everything to end the pain, but nothing works. I'm the problem, I can't stand myself, and I never get a break from being me."

"You seem all right to me." Sally yawned, then pulled her hindlegs into her body until she was sitting up on her haunches.

"You've just met me and almost died because of me. How can you say that?"

The dog shook herself, settling her ruffled coat back into place. "Let's go for a walk and get to know each other then." She stood up and held out a little hand to Katie to help her to her feet.

"I don't think a walk is going to change anything."

"Maybe not, but it might be fun."

Katie looked around at the gloomy sky, the dirty waves of the river below, the dull grey metal and concrete of the city and wondered what enjoyment could be squeezed from such a horrible day.

"Unlikely."

The dog's long, plumed tail beat slowly from side to side.

She extended her paw to Katie, beckoning with her claw tipped fingers. "If not fun, it will certainly be pleasant."

"On a day like this?" Katie raised her eyebrows.

Sally's tongue slipped between her black lips, reminding Katie of pink pulled taffy. "Especially today. Why, there's so much scent carried on the wind. It's glorious."

"Yeah, I'm not big into smells." Katie folded her arms.

"I forgot you can't smell the world as I can. Well, there's the wind to sweep the cobwebs from your mind, and the sky all covered with a blanket to make you feel secure. Don't you just love when the weather is so grumbly and full of promise? You don't know what's to come, but you know it's going to be a good show."

Katie shook her head. She never thought about the weather apart from to curse it. It was always too hot or too cold, too dry or too wet. She looked around at the stormy day from a different perspective. It made her feel small, a tiny piece in a large puzzle beyond her comprehension.

"Come on, Katie. At the very least we'll have each other for company."

She put her hand in the dog's paw and stood up, grunting as she put weight on her left leg. Sally smiled and trotted at her side as they stumbled off the bridge.

A gang of Mustangs, a popular sports star, approached along the footpath. Katie felt her whole body shrink and tense at the sight of them. Some weren't fully augmented, and their original forms flickered like ghosts through the projections.

"Out of our way, indy."

Katie looked away, longing for death once again. The Mustangs started to whoop as they drew closer, preparing their insults.

Sally stepped between Katie and the Mustangs. Her hackles rose in a crest along her back, making her look almost twice as big as she was. The Mustangs slowed, all eyes on the dog. Sally's golden-brown muzzle twitched, her lips peeling back to reveal sharp teeth as long as Katie's fingers.

Silently, the Mustangs crossed to the other side of the road and hurried on their way.

Katie looked at the dog with new respect. Sally trotted on, her glossy black nose sniffing the air intently.

"How long is this walk going to last?"

"Oh, however long you want. Then we can go home and get something to eat. I love food. Then we can have a little sleep. Nothing better than a nice walk, a full belly and a nap."

Katie shook her head. "What if I can't sleep?"

"Why, we'll go for another walk of course. Nothing like exploring to prepare the mind and body for sleep."

Katie couldn't help but laugh at the dog's positive attitude. She reached out and patted Sally on the head. Her fur felt soft as velvet.

"Good dog."

Above them, a spear of sunlight cut through the blanketed sky and edged the clouds with silver.

*

Iseult Murphy currently resides on the east coast of Ireland with five dogs, two cats, a parrot and a couple of humans. When she isn't writing, she enjoys reading, art and spending time with her animals. Iseult's speculative fiction short stories have appeared in over two dozen venues.
More recently she has published two horror novels in the 7th Hell series. Find out more about her at iseultmurphy.com

THE RETURNING
Edmund Stone

Brad stood among the red bandana-ed group of soldiers, the cold wind invading his nostrils, causing him to sneeze, as snot poured over his lip. Bringing a sleeve to ebb the flow, he looked over the leaders, all on horseback, no more able to put an army together than the people they were forcing to join. They showed up this morning, as he emerged from his house, barking orders and pushing. Small men with narrow thoughts, power trips they were unable to stop.

There were four men on the mounts, screaming commands, trying to give this makeshift army some semblance of order, although disorder was all they were accomplishing. It looked more along the lines of madness. It made no sense. No matter what this group of assholes thought, they were all going to die. This motley crew of misfits would probably end up killing each other before they killed anything else. Brad figured the crowd would disband before any fight ensued, fleeing for whatever hole they could find, then be shot in the back, for no other reason than trying to run away.

He didn't care. This world offered him nothing now. Ordering him to do something wasn't needed. The toothless, scrubby man who invaded his house this morning made it sound as though he were resisting, but the truth was quite the opposite. He'd gone willingly enough. Now he contemplated how his death would go, as well as the rest he supposed. Once the night things came upon them, it would be a bloodbath. They'd been stalking the outside perimeter for months now, working on getting into the fresh meat inside. Some of the scouts on the city's perimeter saw them burrowing into the ground. The earth had been rumbling for the past week, Brad figured it was only a matter of time before they made it in. When had they become subterranean?

It was an evolution from when they'd first appeared. Back when the promise of a vaccine was on the horizon. So long ago but then maybe not. Before his wife died, before he was pinned in this city with its mile-high walls. What good would those defenses do now?

Brad wondered if things would've been different if the women, like his wife Adrianna, had lived. The experiment to save humanity. All with the same thing in common, they were recovered drug addicts, needle users. All with the same reaction to the vaccine, immunity from the night things. They held the promise of a new era, the hope to save the next generation from the chaos this world had fallen into.

It all seemed so long ago, the pandemic raged for over a year and a new vaccine was on the horizon, only no one counted on what would happen. When over seventy-five percent of every man woman and child turned into one of those things out there, creatures only coming out at night or lurking in the shadows with a lust for blood. It left the rest of population to suffer the fate of death. Walls were erected to keep the creatures out. Many cities across the world contained what was left of humankind.

So, when all hope was lost for this generation, the great experiment, called Eve, was devised. All the women who were immune to the creatures, would conceive a child, passing their antibodies to them. It was a wonderful idea, filling the world with a promise, a bright spot in a dim future, and it may have worked, save one thing, before the women could give birth, they all died.

Brad and Adrianna were among that group, brought to this city with so much hope and promise. When she became pregnant, she beamed with pride. One of the last things Brad remembered about her along with what she told him, "Brad, hope has been restored."

Even at the time, he wanted to believe her, but doubted. In his eyes, especially now, all he could see was death.

Once the mothers were gone, the experiment to save humanity went with them. Mass graves were erected in the ball stadiums and city parks, all to hide the last hope of humankind.

Now, crammed in, with no hope for the future, they'd become worse than the night things, the ones who wanted to escape weren't allowed. The city had become a prison and the people who tried to go beyond the walls were subjected to torture and horrors unimaginable.

After Adrianna died, Brad retreated to his house, listening to the anguished cries of the escapees near the city walls. Sitting in his basement, drinking the homemade wine he'd stored up, he listened to those poor souls. What had they done wrong? Their only crime to attempt to leave this place of horror for another beyond the wall. All sanity was gone, and Brad wanted no part of it.

That was then and this is now. Standing in the cold, the space of six months he believed had passed since Adrianna died. To Brad's mind, death could not come quick enough. He'd fight the night things of course but knew it would end in his demise. These vaulted warriors would suffer the same fate as all, weeping and gnashing of teeth.

The cold air whipped against his face, the chill of Winter's harshness, of what lay in wait for them, a short season of pain, left to suffer no more. He had to agree with the leaders of the pack though, go out in a blaze of glory, forget all else, take as many as you can. He wondered if they really believed it.

As he stood, his red bandana given him fluttering in the wind, he could feel the ground beneath him tremble. The man beside him began to cry, falling to his knees, crawling across the ground. One of the horseback soldiers came to the position, and reaching down, grabbed the man by the suspenders, hoisting him onto his feet. But it didn't work, the man lost his balance and stumbled forward, landing prostrate on the ground, hands splayed before him. The horseback man in his anger reared the animal and brought the full weight of its front legs onto the man's skull. Brad watched, unmoved by the carnage of the conscripted soldier's head turned to an unrecognizable pulp. This would be mild to what was to come when the night things emerged.

The sky was darkening, and the ground continued to shake, the tremors getting closer. These things didn't bother him either, he was as ready as he'd ever be. His shotgun lay beside him, his knife in his boot and hatchet in his belt. The only weapons he could scrounge when the soldiers came. They were the only weapons he had. The Remington pump and a couple of boxes of shells were all that lay between him and the night things. A futile effort, but one just the same. He may be able to ward off some of the first wave, but if it was anything like the scouts reported, the things were so fast, you'd barely get one shot before ten were on you. Still, what choice did he have? If he were able to stay indoors, they'd break in and take him anyway. No, this was the only way, face them and go out shooting.

Pumping a shell into the chamber, he readied himself for night thing or red bandanaed crazy men, whichever would incur his wrath first. He'd had enough of this world and all the wicked players. Coerced here from his home, now forced to fight in an army he wanted no part of, it was all he could take.

The sun was setting on the top of the hill, and night was fast approaching. The ground was rumbling with more ferocity. The night things smelled the blood and fear surrounding this area and they were hungry for it. The reluctant soldiers were becoming more restless, feeling the dread to come. Brad heard a horse whinny up ahead and then let out a distressed cry, along with the rider. He saw the soldier going down, as the crowd swarmed him and the rest on horseback. They'd had enough of being pushed around.

Instinctively, he stepped backward, slowly making his way from the crowd to an area more suitable to make a stand. When he was near the edge of the group, he heard hoof beats coming fast from behind him - one of the horseback soldiers, trying to push the crowd back to the center, was bearing down on him.

There was little time to do anything, except bring the gun to his hip. The horseback soldier was too close for him to get a proper shot. As the horse ran by him, it knocked Brad off balance and he fell to his side, losing the gun from his grip.

He scrambled for it, but the horse was on him, its hooves digging the ground, trying to overtake him. Then Brad felt the ground violently move around him, pushing him sideways, rippling around like a wave splashing onto a beach.

The horse reared, sending the rider off its back and onto the ground behind it. The horse's nostrils snorted a steam trail visible in the dusky sky. Its eyes were wide, knowing something to be feared was rooting in the ground beneath it. Stepping backward, the beast pushed at the ground, then stutter stepped sideways, before being enveloped by arms jutting from the earth.

The gritty black horde of hands looked like large ants rolling out of mound, as they pawed and grabbed for purchase. The white stallion fell sideways; its feet yanked from beneath it, falling in a violent heap. Night things crawled from the ground and swallowed the beast, ripping its flesh with their teeth and plunging arms into the midsection, pulling entrails out and stringing them across the ground. Their numbers were swelling as they emerged.

The soldier thrown off the horse jumped to his feet and started to run, only to be stopped by several creatures pushing him onto the ground, clawing and digging into the flesh on his back. He howled from the assault, as they ripped

GLIMMER

through him, his clothing becoming bright red.

Brad turned away, looking for an exit, somewhere toward the wall, but there were too many of them. They blotted the landscape as far as he could see. Gunshots were erupting from all around, there was no order, no structured army, the lack of assembly evident, as men and women ran for the wall, only to be knocked down, their bodies desecrated in the blood-soaked field.

He pumped a shell into the Remington and leveled it in front of him, as a creature came barreling toward him. Brad rammed the gun into its mouth and fired. Blood and brain matter exploded from the back of the thing's head. Turning the gun to another direction, while loading another shell, he fired, hitting one of them square in the gut. The thing doubled forward, doing a funny dance, as it writhed on the ground. Pumping another shell into the chamber, he aimed for the things head and ended its movement.

Screams came from behind him, above and below. They were everywhere, so many he couldn't count them all. Howls from the creatures were mingled with the fearful blood curdling screams of the dying. Weeping and gnashing of teeth, Brad thought, just as he knew it would be. He shot another round and kept shooting, hitting as many as he could, but he wasn't making even the slightest dent. The only chance he had was to get back to his house. It was at least a football field distance from here, but it might as well be across the continent, because getting there meant crossing the death field in front of him. If he didn't act fast though there would be no need of even trying.

Shooting round after round, he watched night things fall away, some dying on the spot, others fleeing, rolling on the ground, more insulted than wounded. When he was within fifty feet of the house, his gun went flying out of his hands and into the grass, well out of reach.

A creature leaped for him, but Brad crouched, and the thing passed over him. While down, he pulled the knife from his boot. Then he pulled the hatchet.

GLIMMER

With one weapon in each hand, he ran toward the house. There was still enough daylight left for him to see a wall of creatures hanging from the railings of the porch. Throwing the hatchet, the blade sliced through the air, hitting one of them in the back. It rolled off the railing and into the yard, writhing in agony over the insult of the blade.

Running for the porch, with no gun or hatchet, the only weapon he had was the knife. He held it close, greedily protecting it from being snatched away. Almost to the porch steps, Brad felt the weight of a large group of night things push him forward and onto the porch steps. He whirled around and looked upon the most hideous face he'd ever seen.

Blue veins like interstate roads on an atlas adorned the cheeks and neck of the thing, and its eyes were red and so full of blood they looked ready to burst. The thing chopped at his head, its teeth attempting to gain a bite into the tender flesh of Brad's neck. Managing to free the hand his knife was in; Brad buried the weapon to the hilt under the chin of the crazed beast. It screamed and flailed, knocking several of the things off balance.

Brad pushed off from the crowd and rolled onto the porch, then reached for the door handle, but was dragged backward, as the things pulled at his legs. Kicking with all he had, he hit one of them in the face, cracking bone and causing blood to spout in gushes. This brought on a renewed frenzy, as they tore at each other to get to Brad. Walls of marauders stormed the porch, falling over each other. Hundreds of them pushed and prodded to get to the fresh meal awaiting them.

The horde came crushing onto his body, and he could feel the hands digging at his side and torso, punching furiously at him, his ribs cracking like cinders in a fire. The pain took his breath from him, and with the added weight of the pile, suffocation was only minutes away. He had no recourse now, had fought with what was left of him. Dying on his own front porch didn't seem too bad a way to go.

Brad closed his eyes and waited for his life to be over. Then the weight began to lift.

Brad slowly opened his eyes to the sight of the night creatures dying. A purple light glowed above him, as a clawed hand reached into the bodies of the night things, changing them to dust, the image of the figure intact for a moment, then blowing away with the wind. Several winged creatures were hovering in the sky just above the city streets, childlike cherubim figures, angels or demons, it was hard to tell, but for now, angels fit better.

The one above Brad's porch looked at him for a moment, and he could see something in its eyes, as though a reflection of himself were looking back at him. He considered the creature for a moment. Could it be?

It flew into the sky, fluttering high and low, diving into the crowds of the remaining night things. The rest joined with it and dispatched the creatures in large sweeping lines until they were no more.

Ragged men and women began to emerge onto the street, heading back to their dwellings, disoriented to the happenings around them, but seemingly relieved the fight was over.

The cherubim vanished beyond the wall to eradicate the rest of the night creatures; Brad hoped anyway. Turning for his own house, he opened the door, went inside, and fell face first on the couch, where he slept.

*

As the days passed, the world was cleansed of the night creatures. No one saw any running through the woods or coming out when the skies got dark.

Strangely, the cherubim vanished too. During their short stay, others noticed the same thing Brad did: a resemblance to themselves in the eyes and facial structures of the small heroes. Stranger still, the mass graves where the experimental women were buried, had been disturbed, as small tunnels were dug through the dirt.

GLIMMER

Exhuming several of the women, they all had one thing in common - their midsections were opened, and the babies were missing. More were brought to the surface, and the same evidence presented.

Many people believed the children were incubating in their mother's wombs, waiting for the right time to come to the surface in their new form. Becoming a new species altogether. Either way, they saved humanity from extinction.

In the coming days, Brad would make it his daily ritual to visit his wife's resting place. Laying flowers on her grave, he spoke in soft words, "Thank you, for giving me hope."

*

Edmund Stone is a writer, poet, and artist who spins strange tales of horrifying encounters with the unknown. He lives in a small Ohio River town with his wife, a son, four dogs, and a plethora of cats. He can be contacted at edmundstoneauthor.com, Twitter @edmundstonehwr, or find him on Facebook.

RITUALS FROM BEYOND THE GRAVE
Antonia Juel

Abby lay sprawled on the floor, flipping the pages of the worn old book, when a knock on the door interrupted her reading. She closed the book and sat up—quickly, but not so quickly as to look suspicious.

Her mother Moira entered. "Time for bed, honey." Using the switch by the door, she lowered the lighting to the warm glow of the bedside lamp.

"Is that one of the books left here by Miss Shaw? What's it about?" She nodded to the book in Abby's hands and tugged at a wrinkle in Abby's school clothes, draped over hangers on a hook on the wall.

Abby got to her feet and nonchalantly held forward the shabby, leather-bound manuscript. She had learned long ago that the best way to keep something secret from her mother was to pretend it was nothing special at all.

"*Rituals from Beyond the Grave*?" Moira smiled. "You always find the strangest things, honey. I hope it doesn't give you nightmares."

Abby rolled her eyes. "Mum, I'm eleven years old."

"Even eleven-year-olds can get nightmares." Moira kissed Abby on the top of her head. "Well, don't stay up too late. You know how hard it is for you to get up for school if you don't get enough sleep."

Abby sighed. "Yes, Mum."

The bookshelf in Abby's room, like much of their furniture, had been left by the previous homeowner. Even with all of Abby's books on the shelves, Ms. Shaw's literature took up even more space. Most titles were boring, grown-up tomes about electrophysics and computer technology. Others were works of fiction, which had piqued Abby's interest, but this worn, stained manuscript with the strange title stood out among the lot.

Ten minutes later—teeth brushed, nightgown donned, and book in hand—Abby crawled into bed. The pages were, as the title claimed, filled with rituals, but not all dealt with ghosts and death. Instead, most of the rituals sounded like something Abby would expect to find in a witch's manual, if only witches had existed. How to make your enemy's turnips rot; how to make your enemy's hair fall off; how to summon a horde of leper frogs to your enemy's garden; and other funny spells. The language inside the book was odd and old-fashioned, but she understood most of it. "Thyself," for example, meant "yourself." Her mother sometimes used such words when she quoted stage plays by some dead bloke named Shakespeare.

As Abby worked her way through the unfamiliar writing, she came across a Tesco receipt that seemed to bookmark a page. The receipt appeared entirely ordinary, listing bread, milk, and other groceries, but the page title caught her interest.

How to Cross into The Realm of Death, she read, suppressing a grin. Her mother wouldn't have liked her reading this one. This ritual required beeswax candles, a handful of sea salt, three feathers from a pigeon, a page from a book more than 100 years old, and soap bubbles. Little scribbles filled the margins, written in a tidy handwriting. To Abby's surprise, she recognized the names of three knick-knack shops down in Sussborough: *Mary's Handicraft, Stamps and Stones*, and *Looking Glass*. Whoever had added those comment must have done so in recent time. Looking Glass had opened only a couple of years ago; Abby recalled getting her mother to buy her a paint-by-numbers book on the opening day.

She read the instructions, though she sometimes had to

GLIMMER

go back to read a sentence twice to understand the meaning. The reader—or the *Ritualist*—was supposed to place most of the ingredients—*Reagents*, the book said—in a pile and drip wax upon them. After that, the person had to say some words—an *Incantation*—and blow a bubble.

The last paragraph read: *Repeat the Incantation below while Thou gently placest the Bubble upon the Reagents. When the Bubble poppeth, thy Body wilt fade and Thou wilt step through to the Other Side.*

Abby frowned. Your body will fade? Didn't ghosts usually leave a body behind? A corpse that would need to be buried, while their restless spirit lingered?

She picked up the Tesco receipt. The date said 21st of April last year. The day and month tugged at her memory for a few moments until it occurred to her why. She climbed out of bed and tip-toed over to her desk, where a newspaper cutting sat on her small whiteboard.

Sussborough Woman Missing, read the headline. Abby returned to her bed and tucked her cold feet under the duvet. Even though she already knew what it said, she eyed it again, book resting at her side.

Sophia Shaw, 32, went missing from her home in Sussborough on the night of 23 April. Her colleagues at Sussborough Tech Systems reported she had left work that same afternoon in her usual good mood. When, the next morning, she did not arrive for work, her friend and colleague, Alexandra Thompson, attempted to contact Ms. Shaw. When she had no luck, she instead contacted Ms. Shaw's parents, who upon arriving at their daughter's house, found her missing.

Parents Charles and Rita Shaw have shared with The Sussborough Daily that all doors and windows were locked upon their arrival. Inside, they found a half-finished salad and a craft project on their daughter's work desk, and her work clothes laid out on her bed. Additionally, they said, Ms. Shaw's cat, who is on a special diet, was upset and very hungry.

Said Mrs. Shaw, "Sophia would never abandon Esmerelda. Whenever Sophia needs to leave town overnight, Esme stays with us so we can feed her at regular intervals."

GLIMMER

The rest of the cutting consisted of a request for tips and the contact information of the local police office. Abby chewed her lip. Sophia Shaw had disappeared from this house. She had been the last person to live here before Abby and her mother moved in. Even the furniture in Abby's room had belonged to Sophia Shaw. Eight months after her disappearance, Sophia's parents, lacking space in their small flat, had listed the place for sale, furniture and all. Abby and her mother hadn't owned many things at the time, and were happy to move into the fully furnished house.

Abby read the ghost spell again. The ritual described in elaborate detail how to… well, how to disappear, really. And the scribbles in the margins were in neat, feminine handwriting.

Had this been the book Sophia Shaw read that evening? Could the notes be hers? Abby shivered, the hairs on her arms standing on end.

Once again, Abby looked around the room. Had she not experienced strange things since they moved in? There was that time when her old Mickey Mouse ball had rolled out from under her bed. And that time when she had woken up at 2 a.m. and thought she heard someone crying. And… no, maybe this one didn't count. But her room always seemed to grow colder when she turned off the lights at night.

In the ghost stories she and her friends told to scare each other, it was said that spirits made you feel cold when they passed through you. Could the cold in her room be Sophia Shaw trying to get her attention?

But the newspaper cutting said nothing about salt or candles or old books lying around. Only a salad. Abby was probably just imagining things. She set the cutting aside. The Tesco receipt she put back into the book where she found it.

On the next page followed the ritual *How to Returne*. This spread had no notes in the margins. At the bottom of the left page was a blotch of green ink and a corresponding faint mark on the opposite page. The stain looked old; the edges blurred and faded to a brownish hue.

The first paragraph read: *This Ritual bringeth Thee back from the Other Side. If Thou dost not returne with-in Three Hundred and Sixty-Five days, Thou wilt fade into the Forever Beyond.*

Forever beyond? Abby hadn't heard the phrase before. Did that mean that unless someone brought you back from your ghost-state within a year, you would cease to exist entirely? Maybe she should try to bring Sophia back? Just in case she had accidentally turned herself into a ghost and didn't know how to return. Maybe Abby could save her, even though the police had failed?

The requirements were sea salt, an egg, a glass, a cup of water, a human hair, a *Piece of Writing from the Hand of the Person made Ghost*, and... blood.

Abby grimaced in revulsion. Few of the other spells had used components like blood, though one had mentioned that a frog liver would increase the potency.

She skimmed through the instructions. First, put salt, egg, and hair in the glass, set the glass on the piece of paper, *recite an Incantation*—which meant speaking some words— and last, add the water.

The article mentioned a "craft project" left on Sophia's work desk. What if it wasn't a craft project at all, but the reagents used to perform the ritual?

The next paragraph read:

If Thou lackest an Apprentice, perform the Returne Ritual thyself before Thou leavest. Add One Drop of Blood—Human or otherwise—for each Hour Thou wishest to delay thy Returne from the Realm of Death. Use thine own Blood for greatest Accuracy.

Abby read through the paragraph three times before she understood its message. The blood was a safety measure. It said to perform the return ritual yourself before you leave, because you can't do it with your ghost arms and ghost hands. The number of drops you added would decide how long you stayed a ghost. Four drops would give you four hours and then activate the ritual to bring you back.

Abby frowned. She would be in so much trouble if her

mother popped her head through the door tomorrow morning and saw a ghost take shape before her eyes. If she were to try to get Sophia Shaw back, she had better do it now.

With no blood required, the ritual seemed simple enough. Too simple, in fact. Salt and eggs and water? They had all that available in the kitchen.

But why hadn't Sophia used this ritual to bring herself back? Didn't she want to come back? Abby had heard of people who had killed themselves because they didn't want to continue living. Was that was Ms. Shaw had done?

Then again, wouldn't she at least have left the cat with her parents before she stepped over? And why leave her work clothes out and a salad half-eaten? It didn't make sense. What if she had tried to perform the ritual, but something had gone wrong?

Abby picked up the newspaper cutting again. What was the date?

Sophia Shaw, 32, went missing from her home in Sussborough on the night of 23 April, she read.

Today was the fifteenth of April. Abby counted. Eight more days, and it would be a year since Ms. Shaw's disappearance. Eight more days, and her ghost might fade into the forever-beyond.

"Sophia Shaw?" she whispered, heart pounding. "Miss Shaw, are you there?"

But there was only silence. No one replied in a ghostly voice. No ball came rolling out from under her bed. The windows didn't rattle; the floorboards didn't creak. She didn't notice even the slightest cold brush against her cheek.

Her eyes flew over the ritual again. Three hundred and sixty-five days.

A thought occurred to her. What if Sophia had already started to fade? What if she was too weak to affect the real world anymore? Then she would have no way of letting Abby know she was there.

Abby slipped out of bed. She had to help. At least try. If

she was correct, Sophia was running out of time.

On silent feet, she sneaked out of her room. Tinny voices drifted down the hall from the living room. Her mother was watching a talk show on the telly.

Abby stole an egg from the fridge and put it in her nightgown pocket. She snatched a glass from the dish rack, poured a cup's worth of water in a coffee mug, and squeezed the newly opened carton of salt under her arm. The label said "iodised salt," not "sea salt," but she hoped it didn't matter.

She considered the "Piece of Writing" that had to be made by the ghost person. Could she use the book? Perhaps just a piece from the margins with Ms. Shaw's hand-written notes?

Back in her room, Abby lit the lamp on her desk, tore a small strip of paper out of the margins covered with Sophia's scribbles, and placed the book to one side, open at the page of the ritual *How to Returne*.

With the glass sitting on top of the hand-written note, she pulled a hair from her head, but ended up with three. Ceremoniously, she separated them and put only one of them in the glass, shaping it into a loop along the edge.

She added the salt. Another shiver ran through her when she imagined Sophia Shaw actually appearing in her room, brought back from the other side. What would she look like? A zombie? No, surely not. She was a *ghost*—not *real* dead.

When the last of the white dripped from the shell, she started speaking the words——the *Incantation*.

Body hath Faded, Spirit willeth Roam
Give Breath to the Lifeless, bring Spirit back Home

She repeated the lines a few more times as she poured the water from the mug into the glass, struggling not to spill or mix the words up. Four times, five times, six times, she repeated the rhyme.

Nothing happened.

After her incantation, an eerie silence hung in the air. She

GLIMMER

stared into the dark corners, expecting to see something that would make her run screaming out of the room. Half-transparent shapes, spidery hands, haunted faces.

But there was nothing. No trace of a ghost, woman, or even a zombie.

Her phone lay on the desk with the timer showing 00:00 in flowery font on a pink background. The Minnie Mouse desk lamp Moira had bought her at a flea market grinned happily.

Abby blinked.

What a silly experiment.

What eleven-year-old seriously believed in ghosts? She and her friends loved to tell ghost stories, but no one really believed in ghosts, did they?

She was glad her friends didn't know about her ghost-reviving ritual. At least she had saved herself that embarrassment. She would never speak of this night to a living soul.

The book lay on the desk, taunting her. What a useless piece of rubbish. What had she been thi—

Her eyes snagged on a squiggly line of black in the green discoloration. She narrowed her eyes and took a closer look. What was this? More text? She held the book up to the light.

Yes. An entire paragraph had been all but washed away and then masked by the now-dried, green liquid. Could this be what Sophia missed? Undecided, she stared at the page. Oh, why was she even bothering? The book was just some old witchery theatre prop; she was sure of it.

But... What did this last sentence say? Curiosity overwhelmed her, and after about ten seconds of blinking away tears under the bright lamp light, she had the whole passage.

Stir and drip the Liquid on-to the Piece of Writing. Three Times Thou dost this, and the Ritualist wilt regain their Corporeal Form.

She dropped the book on the desk, where it landed with a soft flop.

Drip the liquid on the writing? Seriously? What

difference would that make? This was a stupid ritual and a stupid book, and Abby was stupid for believing in ghosts in the first place. Sophia Shaw was stupid, too, for disappearing.

The mix in the glass looked like the beginning of one of her mother's disgusting protein smoothies, only missing spinach and broccoli. While the salt was barely visible as a pale powder on the bottom, the egg yolk had broken and leaked yellow goo into the water. The hair wasn't visible, but knowing it was there added to Abby's disgust. What would her mother say if she found all this on her desk in the morning?

She swept up the package of salt and the empty mug. She reached for the cracked eggshell—and paused. The book lay open on the desk. Inviting. Challenging her.

Three drops.

Just three drops.

She sighed.

"Fine. You win. Three drops," she told the book. She glared at the liquid and dipped a finger into the yucky mixture. One drop, two drops, three drops landed on the small strip of paper.

"Are you happy now, book? I did as you said."

She rolled her eyes and spun the chair around to bring the items back to the kitchen.

And her arms turned to jelly.

Salt and mug fell from her hands, but she barely noticed.

Someone was sitting on the floor by her bed. A woman with a black pixie haircut, a t-shirt, and well-worn jeans.

"Hi, Abby." The woman smiled through her tears. "I'm Sophia Shaw. Thank you for rescuing me."

*

GLIMMER

Antonia Juel has one foot in Sweden, one in Norway, but tries to escape the real world by inventing new ones. She draws much of her inspiration from the wild and varied Scandinavian nature, as well as from the lore and history of her ancestors. In her stories you can find gods and ghosts, sentient cats and psychic crows — even the occasional unicorn (though it might be dead).

https://antoniajuel.eu

Instagram: @antoniajuel

CERO MIEDO
Ryan Benson

"Hurry up! Time for the big assembly." Jaquan Porter clapped his hands at the three other teachers at his table. "Lunch is over." He grinned ear to ear.

"What's the rush?" Ron Schultz rubbed his baldhead before gripping his meatball sub with his chubby fingers. "The Superintendent ought to throw us an assembly, not the students. We did the work."

"You don't think the kids deserve credit?" Jaquan shot his empty paper bag into the trash. "Swish! You better hope you're on my team when we hit the court tomorrow, Shane." He high-fived the twenty-something man sitting to Ron's right.

"There's enough credit to go around," said Shane.

"Exactly, Shane-O." Jaquan drummed on the table. Shane, the science teacher, and Jaquan were hired together and had since made it a habit to meet up several times a week to play basketball or grab a beer.

"Yeah, right." Ron smirked. Red sauce ran down his chin. "Because the kids can regurgitate the answers we give them?"

Furrowing his brow, Jaquan stopped drumming.

"It wasn't every student." The fourth teacher at the table, Abigail Conway, chimed in. "Some need a tap, and some need a push."

"And some students need you to pick them up and carry them." Ron noticed the sauce now staining his shirt. "Ah, jeez."

"What are you talking about?" asked Jaquan.

Shane glanced at Ron and then Jaquan. The two friends' eyes met for an instant before Shane turned his attention to his soup.

Abigail laughed in her normal saccharine shrill and touched Jaquan's arm. "You're messing with us, aren't you?"

As if moving in slow motion, Jaquan pulled his arm away. "I have no idea what you're talking about."

A minute later, Jaquan Porter burst from the teacher's lounge and stalked down the school hallway, teeth and fists clenched. As lockers and doors flashed by his periphery, a voice called out from behind him.

"Jaquan," said Ron. "Jaquan!"

Jaquan paid no attention.

Abigail joined in. "Jaquan, wait. Think of the children."

Jaquan stopped in his tracks, causing the man and woman to crash into his back. He spun around to confront the pair. Shane dragged his feet a good ten feet behind them, staring at the linoleum tile.

"I am thinking of the children, Abigail. I can't believe you both allowed them to cheat. Heck, you even helped them cheat."

"We all had to pitch in," said Abigail.

"Our jobs were riding on these little heathens," said Ron. "Don't pretend you didn't cut some corners. Don't give me that 'Caesar Medo' crap you have the kids yelling in the halls."

"It's 'Cero Miedo,'" said Jaquan. "It means 'No Fear.' I make my Spanish class enjoyable and let the students know I'm there for them. You should try that in your math class."

Ron opened his mouth, but Jaquan cut him off.

"I work with the kids after school and grade on a generous curve at times, but I never gave away A's. Cero Miedo is how I challenge the kids to do better. To never surrender. What you both did doesn't help the kids at all."

GLIMMER

"C'mon, Jaquan." Shane had caught up to the group. "You too, man?"

"No." The man again averted his gaze and shifted his weight. "Well, some."

"What?" Jaquan's head hurt from trying to imagine his friend partaking in this scheme.

"Damn it," said Shane. "You know most of these kids won't get anywhere without a little help."

"You aren't helping them. You're helping yourselves."

"And helping you too." Abigail grabbed Jaquan's collar. "This school would have shut down. I have a pension, and I can't start over. Instead, we are all getting awards and citations. I'm the county's history teacher of the year. Monk High School is famous nationwide. Who are you going to tell? Principal Wilson encouraged grade changes."

Jaquan shook his head and pulled Abigail's hands from his shirt. "I'm telling the Superintendent. This isn't right." He looked at Shane. "YOU know it's not right."

Shane cleared his throat. Instead of looking to his feet, he gazed at the ceiling as if searching for a way out.

"Let's talk," said Ron. He looked over Jaquan's shoulder and waved down the hall.

Jaquan turned to see a stocky man standing a head taller than him. He wore Monk High's red and white colors, complete with a hat and whistle.

"Coach Ricketts? I thought you were setting up for the assembly," said Jaquan.

"Abigail texted me. Turn around and go back to the lounge."

"Don't tell me you gave out cheap A's in PE."

"No, but I'm coaching winning football and basketball teams." He pointed at Ron and Abigail. "Thanks to these two, a lot of talented players remained academically eligible."

"High school games are worth your integrity?"

Coach Ricketts chuckled, "I'm getting offers from colleges, Jaquan. I could end up coaching in the pros." The

78

smile left the large man's face. "Don't do anything stupid now."

Abigail muttered to herself and pulled out her cell phone.

"Out of my way," said Jaquan. He grabbed the phone from Abigail and pitched it down the hall.

Ricketts's hand wrapped around Jaquan's arm with a vice grip. Jaquan looked up into the larger man's face. Ricketts's eyes narrowed, and he slammed Jaquan into the lockers. The flesh versus metal crunch echoed down the empty hall.

"Stop it," said Shane.

Jaquan struggled to catch his breath and shook the cobwebs from his head. He bent over before popping up and kicking Ricketts in the crotch. Jaquan made a run, but the doubled over coach grabbed his tweed jacket. The Spanish teacher tried to pull away, but Ricketts reeled him in and applied a rear bear hug.

"Ron, text the principal," said Abigail. Ron stood with his hands over his mouth.

"No worries, I got it." Shane punched the numbers into his phone.

"Please, just stay away from the assembly." Abigail was near tears.

"No," growled Jaquan.

"I'm not getting through." Shane held his phone up, searching for a signal.

Jaquan knew Shane's phone had service all over the school. *First bit of good luck.* As blackness crept in the edges of his view, Jaquan flung his head back, connecting with Ricketts' nose. Blood gushed out, and his assailant hit the floor.

"Aw, jeez," said Ron as he turned away.

Jaquan leaned on the lockers, gasping for air and clutching his side. Abigail berated Ron for his inaction as Jaquan stumbled down the hall towards the gymnasium.

Pain radiated from his ribs up into his head. Jaquan counted the lockers between him and the gymnasium door.

GLIMMER

With ten to go, Principal Wayne Wilson burst out of the door holding his phone. Abigail must have finally gotten to her Nokia.

The principal's frantic face turned a fake brand of happiness when he spied Jaquan.

"Senor Porter! There's my favorite Spanish teacher."

"Save it." Jaquan spat the words out between huffs. "I'm talking to the Superintendent. I'm telling him everything."

Wayne whispered. "Listen here. Abigail texted me about your plans. Think about the kids. You want the seniors to lose their scholarships? Hell, the colleges might flat kick them out before they take a single class. Don't get me started on what will happen to underclassmen." He smiled again. "I didn't want this, but the state demanded results too soon for any real learning to occur. All eyes were on us, and they threatened to pull our funding. We just needed a little more time."

"I'm talking to the Superintendent," Jaquan repeated.

"Fine. Let's ask him." Wayne opened the door and summoned the Superintendent. "Sir, this is Jaquan Porter, one of our finest faculty members."

"Ah, yes." The Superintendent held out a hand but retracted it after it went unshaken by Jaquan. "I was just telling Principal Wilson how impressed we all are about the 'Miracle at Monk High.'"

Buzzing interrupted the three men. Jaquan fished the phone out of his pocket. Why was his wife calling? He looked at Wayne and the Superintendent and pointed at his phone. Wayne smirked as Jaquan answered the phone.

"Jaquan?" the female voice said.

"Trudy, I'm in the middle of—"

"Wayne left me a voicemail. He says you're quitting your job?"

"I never said that." His deep breathing slowed as he stared at Wayne.

"You can't change your career now, Jay. We have plans."

"I know, honey. I have to go." Jaquan hung up before

GLIMMER

Trudy could answer.

"Can we discuss your future after the assembly? I can't wait to get in there and celebrate these kids," said the Superintendent. "You all have a lot to be proud of here at Monk High."

Jaquan looked at the students in the bleachers through the door's glass pane. A din of laughter and chatter escaped the gymnasium.

"Let's go take a seat," said Wayne. He grabbed Jaquan's arm to usher him inside. "We all have a responsibility to the school. We just need a little more time."

Shoulders slumped; Jaquan inched towards the gym. Through the window, he saw the reporters and cameras. He stopped. "You know…"

"Yes?" said Wayne.

Jaquan shook Wayne off his arm. "If you 'just needed more time,' you wouldn't have invited the news." He took another look into the gym and saw the podium at center court. Jaquan inhaled and stood tall. "I have a responsibility to my students—not the school."

The door flew open as Jaquan burst into the assembly. "Hello, Monk High!" The room erupted into a round of cheers. Jaquan strode directly to the microphone. Fred Willis, the English teacher, popped out of his chair, phone in hand. Another Abigail text, thought Jaquan. He bared his teeth and pointed at Fred, sending him back to his seat.

After tucking in his shirt and rubbing his sore ribs, Jaquan snatched the microphone from its stand. It felt good in his hand, like a sword for justice. "I have something I want to say." The students quit talking, and local news reporters and cameras moved closer to him.

Now or never.

After the students graduated, the world wouldn't give them a pass like his fellow faculty members did. Maybe if they gave the kids trust funds and internships at daddy's firm, they would continue skating by, but not as it was.

With an open mouth, Jaquan paused. There, at center

court, sat Lucinda Quinones.

Five colleges, two of them Ivy, accepted her with full scholarships—a feel-good story that went viral. Jaquan was proud to have her as his student and had even written her a letter of recommendation. She worked hard in and out of school. Without a doubt in his mind, Lucinda deserved her place at the top of the class. But how much doubt would everyone else have if the school's dirty secret came out? How much of her future depended on what he said in the next five minutes? Would the media brand every student a cheater?

"I…" The microphone now felt less like a sword in his sweaty hands and more like a bomb. His phone buzzed in his pocket. Wayne and the Superintendent stood in the doorway with Coach Ricketts, Abigail, Ron, and Shane.

And what about himself? Right now, he was innocent, but if he waited for even a second after the assembly, he'd be as guilty as the rest of the faculty. But could he and Trudy make ends meet without this job?

"I wanted to say…" Jaquan's attention returned to his coworkers, which only deepened his indecision. His hands gripped the mic tighter and began to shake until he locked eyes with Shane. The friend Jaquan thought he had lost forever returned, as Shane curled his fingers into a zero and silently mouthed, 'Cero Miedo.'

Jaquan inhaled and closed his eyes. *No fear.*

Time for the disservice to end. Lucinda had earned her grade. All his students did—and they'd earn their success in the real world, too.

"Ladies and gentlemen. I have something to say."

*

Ryan Benson previously found employment as a researcher/professor in Boston, MA. He now resides outside of Atlanta, GA with his wife

GLIMMER

and children. Ryan hopes to one day complete a novel, but until then he keeps himself busy writing short fiction stories. The Sirens Call Publications, Trembling With Fear (Horror Tree), ARTPOST, Dark Moments (Black Hare Press), Short Fiction Break, and the anthology The Collapsar Directive (Zombie Pirate Publishing) have published his work.

NIGHT SCAR
W. E. Pearson

Annie Malone woke from the dream again. The recurring one that haunted her for years.

She reached to touch her throbbing head. That told her that the nocturnal creatures had made a new incision in her brain, as she slept. Annie had recurring memories of these beings. They were slender and translucent, with rainbow-colored halos around their heads.

Reaching for her gun from the night table, she stealthily checked the apartment. But no one was ever there, only in her mind and only in her dreams. That's when they came to alter her surgically implanted program chips in her brain.

For the first time, Annie's new programming gave her some clues surrounding the day she was born. Her biological father abandoned her at birth and her mother refused to talk about it—no wonder she became a detective. This chip allowed her mind to travel backward and forward in time. Tonight, she would run the program to find out more. Her hope always was to connect with her father.

Annie started the coffee maker, hopped in the shower, and drank her coffee while dressing. She slid her gun into her custom-made belt.

She looked into her full-length mirror, focused, and began an x-ray-vision scan of her entire body. The results confirmed it. There was a new scar on the right side of her brain.

The voice tutorial told her she could now diagnose

deadly diseases. The newly implanted chip must be an upgrade.

What she didn't know was what new ability the chip would activate. Or when it would happen. Fear was the trigger that switched it on, but she learned quickly how to regulate her new power.

Taking deep breaths, she attempted to calm herself.

Her fellow homicide detective, Marcus Berger, thought she was strange from the moment they met. They joked about it now, having been partners for years. Both of them had grown to rely on each other. For detectives, that code of trust was a matter of life or death.

Numerous times she had used her superpowers to scan buildings when they sat for hours doing surveillance. Her famous, "I have a 'gut feeling' that somebody is armed and inside," camouflaged her powers. Many cases were solved because of her ability alone–knowing how many armed bad guys were inside a building gave them a big advantage. This saved lives. Her partner came to trust Annie's instincts. If she said they needed to ask a possible suspect to open his car trunk, then he knew they would find drugs, illegal weapons or even worse.

*

Marcus and Annie arrived and parked, simultaneously, at the Cincinnati Police Department.

"Did you have a fun weekend?" asked Marcus as they entered the building, heading for the morning staff meeting.

"Uneventful," lied Annie. "How was yours?"

"Pretty good."

Two smart-ass cops they had some run-ins with made their way past them to find seats. "Hey, 'silver bullet,' said one of them to Marcus, referring to his tied-back gray locks.

Marcus flipped the guy 'the bird'.

"What about you 'eagle eyes'?" said the other one.

Annie stared him down. "I see you're going commando

today, ass-wipe," she said. That made the guy double check to make sure he had his boxers on.

The staff sergeant updated the group on new cases, as the lieutenant assigned weekly tasks. He ended the meeting with, "Go catch those bad guys."

*

Marcus grabbed a folder. "Let's tackle our top priority case. Okay?"

"Sure thing, I'll get coffee." Her long raven-black ponytail caught the back of his chair as she walked by, so Marcus gave it a little tug to release it.

"I think your tail can double as a weapon," he joked.

"One of many I possess," quipped Annie.

*

"This killing of a local eight-year-old girl, Cassie Summers, is eating at me."

"Me too," said Annie. "How did the abductor grab and kill her within a one-hour time frame, and then dump her body in a shallow grave only five miles from her home? We need to push for that coroner's report."

"Let me read you the statement from Mr. and Mrs. Summers," said Marcus.

Cassie Summers and her ten-year-old brother were riding their bikes
on some makeshift ramps in an abandoned parking lot in the neighborhood. Skateboarders built the ramps to practice their sport.

Cassie wanted one more turn at it, but Tommy told her he was going home and left.

One of the Summers' neighbors was driving home from work, past the parking lot, when he spotted a young girl being dragged, kicking and screaming into a blue van. The vehicle sped off in the other direction, then vanished before the neighbor had a chance to intervene or get a close look at the child or the abductor.

Annie grabbed the file off Marcus' desk to look at the crime investigator's photos. "Let's check out the kill site. We need to see it for ourselves since we're heading up this case."

*

As Marcus parked, he recognized the area from the case photos. The whole perimeter was cordoned off with police tape. The file indicated that the crime investigators had been to the site and collected all possible evidence. This allowed them to walk the entire area, without disturbing anything. They noticed a wooded area adjacent to the kill zone.

They both bent down to examine the dried blood in the shallow grave where Cassie's body was dumped. Marcus heard a noise and raised his head in the nick of time to shout, "Wolf! Look out!"

Reaching for his gun, he stood, frozen; as time stood still.

Fear hit Annie's brain like a lightning bolt as she sensed power release. The new ability activated, and three duplicates of herself surrounded the wolf, confusing the animal. Clone one took an x-ray-vision scan of the wolf. The results popped up on her mind screen. Shapeshifter Assassin. Mission failed. Wolf vaporized by the sender.

Annie stood two feet from Marcus as the clones vanished, as though dismissed. Suddenly, Marcus could move—only to find he was aiming at nothing.

"Are you alright, Annie?" Marcus asked.

But her mind was on the new chip upgrade. Once she ran the program tonight, it would fast track her on time travel and how time freezes.

*

On the drive back to the station, Annie's phone rang.

"Hello. Yes, I'm Annie Malone. What? What happened?" Her stomach clenched, and her heart pounded. Her throat tightened, so she reached for the bottle of water on the floor to take a swig. "Where are you taking her?" Annie demanded? "Is she unconscious? I'll meet you there."

"Hey," said Marcus gently. "You okay? Who's unconscious?"

"My mother is. She fell and banged her head at a neighbor's house. The ambulance is en route to UCMC Hospital."

"What happened?"

"She's been having frequent falls. The worst part is that she refuses to go to the doctor. Every time I visit her, she's got more bruises. I'm sure she's experiencing mini strokes but is in denial."

A glimmer of hope flashed through Annie's mind as she remembered the new chip upgrade. Now she could do a full x-ray-vision scan on her mother at the hospital to diagnose her condition.

"Hey, Annie, are you having one of your premonitions again? Is she going to be alright?"

Annie's phone interrupted them. "Hello. What? My mother's vital signs are gone? Are you positive?" she cried. "Try to revive her. I'm on my way."

The car froze on the road. The sun stood still in the sky, and the moon stopped. Marcus sat motionless like a statue. She felt power release from her body like a cannonball releasing from the barrel of a cannon. Uh-oh, she sensed, as three clones activated.

The chip pulled a screen up in her mind. Clone one was at the hospital. Her squeaky shoes made an eerie sound on the tiled floor of the hospital as she dashed amongst the frozen doctors and nurses to find Annie's mother. An image of her mother's serene and peaceful face transmitted on her screen.

Clone two picked up Cassie's autopsy report from the coroner's office and transmitted her a copy. She looked like a ray of sunlight as she speed-skated around the still-like morgue staff.

Annie saw and sensed Clone three's hand reaching for a letter at her mother's house, even though her fingers were clenching the armrests in Marcus' car. The screen projected her mother's image, voice, and words:

Dear Annie,

> *If you're reading this letter, then I'm dead. Your father is an alien surgeon from the Arcturus race in the constellation of Orion.*
>
> *The superpowers are his ongoing gift to you.*

Love, Mom.

Tears of sorrow and joy rolled down Annie's face as she dismissed the clones with the blink of her eyes.

*

W.E. Pearson is a fiction writer. Her first novel, a middle school/YA book is queued to be edited. Currently, she's in third draft rewrites with her second novel and hopes to publish it next year. She's also working on her third novel. She writes in several different genres (Fantasy, Sci-Fi, Mystery/Thriller, Children, Horror and Literary fiction). Some of her short stories have been published on Short Fiction Break and Horror Tree. Since 2015, she has helped to moderate an online writing forum.

DEEPER THAN LOVE
David Rae

"Friends can be deeper than lovers, friendship deeper than love." I read that in a book somewhere.

Yeah right. I don't think so. I've never cried because some friend wouldn't speak to me, or because someone I used to hang with won't answer my calls. I've never felt my stomach muscles clench and my heart race like a trapped animal because I had a great conversation with my girlfriend in the checkout line.

I've never woken up in the middle of the night and wondered what would have happened if I had stayed in touch with my high school friends, or if perhaps I'm running in the right circles and need to move on.

No, it's when your lover won't answer your calls, or when you see someone that you know you want. It's when you ask yourself where your first love is now and how something so brilliant could end so badly. Or it's when you wake up at night looking at the man next to you and think what the hell am I doing with you? That's what's deep.

We tell lovers things we tell no one else. We show them things that no one else gets to see. Do things for them we would not do for anyone else. Things they make us do, never mind if we want to or not.

*

How did I get here? It's a question I ask myself. All alone

GLIMMER

with nothing except my suitcase. I'm walking through the city, I don't know where I'm going or what I'm doing. I only know I'm not going back. I can't. I couldn't go back even if I wanted to.

Sure the concierge would let me in. He might even smile and doff his cap. Right now I must look like a tourist. A pretty girl dressed up and dragging a case, what else would I be. No one would think I was a runaway, an escapee, a fugitive.

I don't go fast. He's not going to come after me. I don't have to worry about that. That's all over. He will never treat me that way again, not ever.

The suitcase wheels click as I walk along the sidewalk. Where am I going? I don't know, I don't have a plan. I look around me and I'm not even sure where I am. How long have I been walking? It doesn't seem that long. Where's the street sign? There's a junction up ahead. I walk and can't help feeling that I'm being watched. 142nd Street, a long way from midtown. No wonder my feet are sore.

I think about calling a cab, but where to? It's a question I can't answer. Besides, now I don't have so much money. I took all the cash that was in the apartment, but I left the cards. They were in his name anyway. If I used them, I could be traced. I learned that from watching *The Hunt is On*. Who said TV never gave you an education.

There is some kind of play area up ahead. Just shows you how far I've gone. Kids, who thought there were kids in Manhattan? Anyway, there's a seat I can sit on so I'm grateful for that. Take a load off. My feet are killing me. I should have worn sneakers instead of these shoes. But these are my favourite pair. I couldn't leave them behind.

I draw out a cigarette and light it.

"Hey, what are you doing, you can't smoke here."

Some do-gooder comes over, a man.

"This is a playground, our kids' lungs live here and they don't want your smoke."

That does not even make sense. But I put the cigarette

out anyway. The last thing I need is more hassle. I look up at him from my seat. He's short, fat, bald and scruffy. He's dressed out as if he shops at Target. He's prissy and I watch as one of the kids comes over. The kid is like him, chunky.

I get up and grab the suitcase. Keep moving, like a bag lady. Keep moving, there's no place for you here. No place for me anywhere. At some point, I'm going to have to find a place to set things down. The case weighs a ton. I don't know how much longer I can drag it around.

*

I'm better off on my own. I always have been. Men just hold you back, hold you down. It's been like that since high school. A pretty face is as much a curse as a blessing.

One guy I knew asked me why pretty girls always go out with jerks. I guess he was asking why I wasn't going out with a nice guy like him. Why don't pretty girls go out with losers like him? But the real reason is because all men are jerks, every last one of them. They seem all so nice, to begin with, but once you're with them it's like they own you. Well, no one owns me. No one.

*

When I met Tod, he seemed different at first, but then they all do. He had a nice smile. That's what attracted me to him first. I was out with my gals, and he came up to me and smiled.

"Hi gorgeous, what are you doing here?" Not that original, but he had this goofy smile that made me laugh. It was like, what else could he say. I told him I was there with friends.

"Okay, but not boyfriends?" No, not boyfriends.

"So maybe I could call you?" I think I gave him my number just to get rid of him, but he was hot. And well

GLIMMER

dressed. I could see he was wearing a genuine Rado on his wrist. And his dental work must have cost thousands. So I gave him my number, why not? I gave Tod my number, and when he called I answered.

*

"Girl, the rate you go through men, you better give them all your number." Yes, not nice. Tracy said that. Well, she got what she deserved. And she said she was my friend too.

*

He took me out, and we had fun. I mean, Tod was good looking, we made a cute couple. We had a blast, we had a laugh. And when he called me again, I thought why not? He had money, had class. It looked as if I had finally struck paydirt. Got me a man with looks and money. I could tell he was really into me. And yes, I was into him too.

Those eyes, and that hair, and that... Well, never mind that.

I started staying over at his place. Nothing was said, nothing decided, but more and more of my stuff ended up at his place. At first, it was just the odd night here and there. Then the weekends and then, what was the point in paying rent on my crummy place, when I could stay in an apartment in midtown?

It was some apartment too, the sort of place you see in those magazines. It was big and bright and airy with a fabulous view. There was a great kitchen, but to be honest neither of us were much into cooking. Tod pretty much lived off protein shakes, and I don't eat much. There's a price for looking this good.

Mostly we were out anyway. I'm not sure what Tod did during the day. We never spoke that much when we were alone. I think he was some kind of fancy lawyer, but he had contacts too, good ones. The kind that got you into parties, the kind of parties you wanted to go to. I met a ton of guys in the business. Tod said he wanted to set me up. I can dance and sing. And I can act. All I needed was the right break and these guys could make my dream come true.

I shouldn't name names. They never came right out and said them anyway, but I knew who they were. I had pictures on my phone. But I didn't need to look them up online. There was always someone saying, do you know who that is? And they always wanted to meet me. Why wouldn't they? I was always the classiest girl there.

Of course, they were looking for pay-back. I can always tell by the way they look at me. It's part of it. Goes with the territory. I know his name. Tod introduced us.

"Whoa, where did you pick her up?" he asked Tod.

Tod smiled. "She's great, isn't she?"

"What are you boys talking about?" I pretended I didn't know. But I knew. I looked at Tod.

"It's okay, babe," he said, "There's a room."

I don't want to think about it now. It made me mad at the time, but what else could I do? I smiled and followed Tod and Mr X, the big shot.

That room.

"You want this, don't you," said Tod. And I suppose I did, just not that way.

Afterwards, we went back out and mingled. Did they even know what happened, maybe they did. The place was full of girls just like me. They all wanted something, all filled with hope. It's then that it hit me. *They're not looking to help us, they are looking to help themselves. They don't care about us. Not even Tod. He's just using me. They're just using us. They're taking our hopes and dreams and using them against us.*

I never thought that Tod was The One. I never thought of us growing old together, but I thought I meant something to him. I held his hand and smiled up at him. When he turned and smiled back I could see all his teeth and his eyes. I saw exactly what he was. Not a big shot lawyer, just a high-class pimp. I was his girl alright. He had caught me and now

GLIMMER

I was his.

*

There's no point thinking about that now. I knew what I was getting into. No time for feeling sorry for myself. That's all over and done with now. I can't sit here forever so I get up and start dragging that suitcase behind me. Clickety-click the wheels go.

"Excuse me, ma'am," some black guy shouts. "Are you lost?"

He comes over. I'm not afraid.

"You got far to go? That looks heavy."

I make up a hotel in Hudson Heights.

"You got a ways to go. You should get a cab. Good luck with that in this neighbourhood."

He offers to take my case for me. I shake my head; what if he runs away with it. Not that he'd get far pulling this weight.

"I'm ok," I say. "It's not that far. And really it's not that heavy."

Now that I get the chance to look at him, he's younger than I thought, and not bad looking. He's got one of those fez caps that Muslims wear. He smiles at me, and he's not bad looking at all.

"I can't leave a lady in need," he says.

That's kind of him. It takes a few minutes to persuade him I'm alright. He's not threatening or anything. In fact he's kind of sweet in a serious way. Religious people often are. I wonder what he'd think if he knew the truth about me. They're always sweet until they find out. He bows to me politely before he lets me go on my way.

*

When I reach the bridge, I'm kind of shocked. I guess in a way I knew this was where I was headed. Where else could

GLIMMER

I go? The south pedestrian way is closed for repairs. So I have to go under the road and up the other side. It's late now, maybe seven o'clock and the sun is beginning to drop from the sky. It's quite a view. I'm looking over to New Jersey. Looking up the river, I can see The Palisades on one side and Hudson Heights on the other.

There's a sign on the bridge, actually lots of them. Maybe one every fifty yards. THINKING ABOUT SUICIDE? CALL THE SAMARITANS. FREE PHONE NUMBER OR USE THE FREE PHONE AT THE CROSSING BOOTH. If I hadn't been thinking about suicide before, then I am now. The signs are everywhere. I *am* thinking about suicide. The handrail is only a few feet high -it would be so easy to get over it. I wonder what it would be like. A few moments of ecstasy, like flying and then it's all over. Would it really be that easy, just to end it all?

I think of Tod and what he did to me. How he used me. But I won't give up. I won't do it, I tell myself. I won't let them beat me. I won't let them win. I'm better than they are. After last night and all that happened. Who could blame me if I did? But I won't. *I'm stronger than you, Tod, I showed you that already. Even after all you did, I got my own back. I won't throw that away now.*

I stop in the middle of the bridge. This is what I have come for. Just do it and get it over with. Before I know it, I'm gripping the handrail and hoisting my case over. The case weighs so much. It must be heavier than I am. But I don't give up.

I get it over the edge and it dangles there for a few moments. Let go, let go, I tell myself. I can feel the weight of it pulling on me, pulling me over. I'm gripping the handrail and bracing myself to stop me from being pulled over. It seems like forever, that case hanging there pulling at me, drawing me over. It would be so easy just to let it drag me down. It wouldn't be that bad. Who would miss me? *Not Tod*, I say to myself and bitter laughter rises up. I'm laughing to myself and the sound of it is the creepiest thing

I've ever heard. It's as if I'm not really here, like someone else is laughing. *Is it you Tod, are you laughing at me? Well, too bad, because you won't win.*

Let go, let go, a voice in my head is screaming. My arm is aching with the pain of holding the case, but my fingers won't open. I'm not sure how much longer I can hold on. I close my eyes and breathe deeply. *You can do this.* One by one, my fingers slip, and suddenly the case is falling. I watch it tumble down into the Hudson. That could have been me. Now I have no desire to follow it. To follow him.

I step back from the edge. Time has restarted.

"Goodbye, Tod," I say as I see the case splash into the river and sink below the surface. Finally, he is gone. How far does he sink; deeper than lovers, deeper than friends. Deep into the water and the mud. Deep below the surface. He won't be coming back. It's over. He was not The One, we are finally over. He's gone.

Not to worry, there are plenty more fish in the sea, or in this case, the Hudson.

*

David Rae's dark fantasy novel CROWMAN will be published in the autumn by press. You can read more of his work at https://davidrae-stories.com/ or follow him on Facebook at https://www.facebook.com/Drdvdrae/ His Amazon page is https://www.amazon.com/David-Rae/e/B07F3H1RND/ref=sr_ntt_srch_lnk_1?qid=1549441677&sr=8-1

SIX STEPS FORWARD
D.A. Steen

The guards dragged me, shackled and chained, down the dimly lit corridors of Holman Prison. For two years they had incarcerated me in the general population wing while my case worked its way through the courts. Now, with the last of my appeals denied and my murder conviction upheld, the warden ordered me transferred to Death Row—the wing of the prison the inmates here called the Slaughterhouse.

I tried to stand, but the guards wouldn't have it. Past sullen-eyed sentries they hauled me, yanking me through two-inch-thick, steel-door security checkpoints and down long winding hallways, shredding the skin on my backside. If I had learned anything after two years in Alabama's most violent prison, it was how to endure suffering. I tried focusing on anything but the agony and watched with growing trepidation as the architecture of the hallways retrogressed from modern 1970s concrete walls to damp, moldy bricks that looked like something out of the 17th century.

They dropped me at the foot of an arched gateway and presented the papers officially transferring me to my new home on Death Row. The gateway looked more like the entrance to a dungeon than to a prison block. An inscription above the archway read: Through me you pass into the City of Woe. As inspiring a quote as I could recall, I recognized it from the Divine Comedy as the inscription Dante found carved above the gateway to Hell. It was apropos to this heinous place, I thought, for few who passed beyond this gate would ever leave alive. The Slaughterhouse, indeed.

Minutes later, they dumped me on the floor of a dingy prison cell that smelled of urine and feces and something I couldn't place—death, perhaps. Well past lights-out, the cell floated in a darkness so thick I could just make out the outline of a bed, a sink, and a toilet.

"Welcome to the Slaughterhouse, Aikens," one of the prison guards said. He grunted and kicked me in the head. The other laughed and as he reared back to kick me, said, "This is from the Reverend," though in my stunned confusion I could have sworn it was the Reverend's voice I heard.

My midsection bent from the crunching blow. The sound that rang out was like a stepped-on stick snapping in two. Something in my ribcage cracked, and I winced in misery.

The Reverend.

The very thought of him was like acid in my mind.

Unable to scream, I fell into silent anguish. The guards slammed shut the heavy steel door of the cell, and the echoes that reverberated down the long cell block rang out with ominous finality.

An acrid acceptance washed over me; my fate sealed; sentenced to die in the electric chair. No one was coming to save me. How masterfully the architect of my fate had played his hand: the goddamned Reverend. I recalled the night Anna introduced us. When she had turned away, I thought I glimpsed a flicker of callousness in his eyes, an uncaring for her that bordered on contempt. But he blinked and it was gone, replaced with a crooked smile. And I doubted what I'd seen because he was a man of God—and her father. If I had only known then what lay beneath his icy veneer, I would have killed him.

Blood from my forehead dripped on the concrete like water dripping from an old rusty faucet.

My thoughts returned to that night two years before when I stood holding Anna, the horrific sound of her blood dripping to the floor, her body gone limp like a wilting flower—until she slid from my arms and lay still.

On the frigid prison concrete, I labored to breathe. The broken rib prevented me from getting full breaths. I was so very tired. It occurred to me then, I could just stop breathing. I could end the suffering.

It took a few attempts, but I found the longer I waited between breaths, the easier it was to forget to take the next one. Until finally, I slipped over the edge and fell into black.

Then came a whisper so close I could feel its breath upon my ear.

"Six steps forward."

I jerked upright, shocked back into my skin. "Who said that?"

"Three steps across."

My eyes darted to every dim corner of my cell, but no one was there.

"Six steps back, turn and restart."

The voice seemed to come from everywhere and nowhere at once. And though it was startling, there was a calmness in the man's voice I found comforting.

Had I imagined it? Was I dead?

"Six steps forward, three steps across. Six steps back, and what have you lost?"

I studied the stone wall separating my cell from the next one over, now suspecting the voice belonged to the prisoner in the cell next to mine. Though I had no idea what he was going on about, he spoke as if a friend. Still, I had to remember where I was. For in the City of Woe, we were all killers and ghosts.

"Listen, I haven't had the best of nights. I'd like to be left alone."

My new neighbor slid across the smooth concrete floor to the front of his cell. "Brother, forget about those backwoods country guards. No one will hurt you here. Not

GLIMMER

on Death Row. The guards here are a superstitious lot. They think it's bad mojo to mess with the ones about to die. They stay as far from us as they can. They're afraid we will come back and haunt them."

I laughed. Just enough to prod my stinging ribs. I liked the sound of whatever this guy was selling.

The voice from the dark shuffled his way back into the inner recesses of his cell.

"You go on now and get some rest. Your wounds will heal. We have to make sure your spirit does, too. Tomorrow, we'll take a walk down by the river. You will feel much better. You'll see."

I didn't know what to make of my new neighbor. He sounded like an intelligent man, sagely even. But the nearest river was forty miles away. And I had seen the fenced-in recreation area outside for those on death row. It wasn't much bigger than a batting cage. Oh well, he may not be all there, but at least he seems friendly enough. In a place like Holman Prison, that is no small thing.

"By the way," he said, "the name's Miles. Miles Monroe."

I blinked several times. "I'm Arthur. Arthur Aikens."

The next day I slept till noon and was pleased to find a tray of breakfast on the floor of my cell. Four strips of bacon and a small serving of scrambled eggs later, and I was feeling life return to my aching body.

"Are you ready?"

It was the voice from the dark.

"Ready for what?" I asked skeptically. "To take that walk you mentioned?"

Miles laughed. "The guards only let us outside three times a week for fresh air and exercise. It will be tomorrow or the next day before you will get your hour out in the prison yard. With those injuries of yours, I was thinking it may do you some good to move about some."

"You mean in here? In this cramped cell?"

"That's what I'm saying."

GLIMMER

I scoffed, glancing around, shaking my head.

"I'll do it with you," he said. And I could hear him stirring in the cell next to me. "Start at the front of your cell. Walk towards the back until you come to the toilet. Turn, shuffle three steps towards the bed, then turn again and walk back to the front. Lather. Rinse. Repeat."

Then it hit me, and I couldn't stop myself from calling out, "Oh! Six steps forward. Three steps across. And six steps back?"

Like a piano maestro hearing his student play through his first composition, I heard the pride in Miles's voice saying, "and what have you lost—by trying?"

And though I couldn't see him, I knew he was grinning.

I had to admit, the man's good-natured disposition toward this walking thing was infectious. What the hell, I thought.

So, we walked—him in his cell and me in mine. And while it took a little getting used to, before long I found I was enjoying it. Soon, I lost myself in thought. Six steps forward. Three steps across. Six steps back. Turn and restart. The phrase began to percolate in my mind and seemed not to just be instructions for taking a walk in one's cell, but perhaps a mantra for surviving this place. For not giving up—which I very nearly had.

And that is when it happened the first time.

"I like the old Cherokee walking trail, you see," Miles said from over in his cell. "Runs here alongside the Tennessee River a good five miles. The river is muddy today. They got a lot of rain up Chattanooga way, you know. River's choppy. A little too windy for my taste, but it keeps most of the mosquitoes away. They can be a might bothersome in this muggy July weather we're having."

While he spoke, I began to see the river. I began to feel the heat of the sun on my skin—to smell the mist of river water taken aloft by the whitecaps and wind. I felt the tickle of a mosquito land on my arm and looked down. No sooner had I caught sight of the little bugger did it sink its proboscis into my flesh. A gust of wind sent it tumbling into the ether and damned if I didn't find myself grateful for the wind. Meanwhile, Miles had kept walking and I had to trot to catch up.

"Now we're entering the old-growth part of the trail," he said, "a dense forest that runs alongside the river. And it's filled with critters."

As soon as Miles spoke, the hoot of a great horned owl called out in the distance. Squirrels scurried across the duff—chipping and chirping. Dozens of bird species came to life, bobwhites, blue jays, sparrows—whistling and singing their songs. Even a mourning dove hummed its soulful song from out on the fringes.

I don't know how long I kept walking down that trail, but at some point, I realized Miles had stopped talking. Just like that, the river, the trees, and the trail, all disappeared. And there I stood, in my dreary gray prison cell, eyes wide and mouth agape.

"W-what just happened?"

"Why, whatever do you mean, Mr. Aikens?" Miles asked wryly from over in his cell.

"I-I could have sworn we were there, walking alongside the river. It was so real!"

And although I couldn't see him, I could feel Miles grinning. It wasn't until later that I noticed the mosquito bite on my arm.

After that, we walked nearly every afternoon. I developed a blister on my heel as we walked along the Appalachian Trail in the Smoky Mountains. I became dizzy while hiking along the canyon rim at the Grand Canyon and had to sit for a spell—heights aren't my thing. And after we walked through the desert in Joshua Tree National Park and returned to Holman, I had a sunburn on my arms and sand in my prison shoes.

Anywhere Miles had been in real life, he could spirit walk, as he called it. And while I returned with such things as a sunburn or sand in my shoes, I quickly learned bringing

GLIMMER

back living things was strictly forbidden. After trekking beneath the California Redwoods one afternoon, we made our way into Fern Valley and sat and talked for a while. Before we left, I picked a piece of fern to take back with me to my prison cell. I went to stuff it into my jacket pocket but felt the firm grip of Miles's hand on my wrist.

"We mustn't ever travel with any living thing on our person, Arthur. Not in our hands. Not even in our pockets."

"Why?" I asked, surprised at the intensity of his insistence.

"Travel with a leaf and the tree from which it came would die. Those ferns in Fern Valley could all come from the same plant. Travel with that little piece of fern and you could kill all of Fern Valley."

I gently laid the fern on the ground and stepped away.

Sunday was Visitor's Day at Holman Prison. My sister would usually come and spend a half-hour giving me updates about my niece and the world outside. Once, I saw Miles in the visitor's receiving area. He was in the corner, sitting across from a young woman I assumed was his daughter. Miles's eyes never left her face. It was as if he didn't want to miss a single moment of her speaking. Late that evening, in the darkest stretch of the night, I heard Miles in his cell. He was sobbing.

All things eventually end, and today would be my last day with Miles. Tomorrow they will execute him. I figured we would travel somewhere special, being Miles's last free day and all. Just after lunch, as was our custom, I started stretching my legs to prepare for our walk.

"Psst," I heard from the front of Miles' cell.

I crouched over in the corner of my cell to get closer. "What is it?"

"Why don't you do it today?"

"Do what?" I asked.

"Lead us on a walk."

"How?"

Miles tossed a copper penny down in front of my cell.

104

GLIMMER

"I've had that penny for two years now. There is enough of me infused into that penny to allow you to use my gift at least once. Go ahead. Give it a shot."

"Wh-what do I do?"

"Just think about somewhere you've been. Recall the smells from that day. The temperature outside. Where the sun was in the sky. Clutch that penny tightly in your hand and think yourself there, walking where you want to be. Then start walking. You can do it."

A few steps later and—just like that—we were there, back on the Tennessee River on the Cherokee trail where Miles had first taken me on a spirit walk.

Miles laughed and turned to me with a big, confused smile on his face. "What are we doing back here? I thought for sure you would want to go somewhere a little more... exciting?"

I shook my head. "No, this is perfect. I like this trail. It is quiet, pretty, and it's home."

Miles smiled. The two of us had come full circle, and with a little mist forming in his wizened eyes, he nodded in appreciation.

We walked, and as we neared the old-growth section of the trail, I asked the question that had been nagging at me.

"Miles, if you don't mind me asking, how did you end up on Death Row?"

He stopped walking, looked down at his old brown leather wingtips, and sighed. Then, with a face heavy with the weight of regret, he lifted his gaze until his eyes met mine.

"I killed my wife, Arthur."

I blinked. I had come to revere Miles Monroe as a near angelic being. In Holman Prison, I had even thought of him as my angel. Sent to guide me out of this hellhole to a place beyond the pale blue sky.

"It's true, Arthur. I'm not proud of it, but I have accepted the truth of what I did. One night I came home terribly upset about something. I had been drinking heavily, something I hadn't done since I returned home from Vietnam. My wife, Doreen, tried to help my stumbling ass make it to the couch, but I guess I tried to push her away. She tripped over the ottoman and fell and hit her head against the radiator. She died on the spot. I have never forgiven myself and I am ready to take my seat in the electric chair. God willing, I'll get to see her again to tell her how sorry I am. I loved that old woman. She was good to me."

He looked frail. I had never seen him look so human. "I'm sorry, Miles."

My angel battled his emotions, blinking back tears until he found himself and straightened. "Well, how about you, Arthur? How did you get on Death Row?"

"You don't know? It was in all the papers."

"I heard we had a famous wife-killer coming to the row, but I didn't hear any details."

I sighed. "Well, I'm like you, Miles. I killed my wife."

Shock registered across Mile's face. "I thought you were going to say you were innocent. You don't seem like the kind of man who would kill his wife, Arthur."

"Neither do you, Miles."

"Touché," he said, rubbing his beard. "Go on."

I motioned to a trail bench and we sat.

"Well, I fell in love with a preacher's daughter. Except, he was more than a mere preacher. The Reverend is a preacher on television who rules over an empire. He's made millions. Turns out, he preaches a lot about love, but he doesn't much believe in it. He thought I was marrying his daughter for her money. But I would have married Anna even if she were penniless.

"Twice, the Reverend had his thugs beat me up. He threatened to kill me if I didn't stop seeing her. But that only made Anna more determined, and we were married in secret. Later that night, I dropped her off on the street behind my house so she could sneak in the back way in case any of her father's thugs were watching. I drove around the block and parked the car in the driveway. Inside, I crept to my room where floor to ceiling windows overlooked downtown Birmingham. There was just enough light for me to see Anna step from the shadows. We kissed. And I'll tell you, Miles, we had ourselves a moment. I won't say it was spiritual, maybe not even profound. But it was ours. And it was supposed to last for the rest of our lives. For a few seconds, it did."

I looked up to see tears forming in Miles's eyes.

"I heard what sounded like a crack in the glass of the picture window and Anna went limp in my arms." My voice broke. "And she was gone. The bullet was meant for me, you see. They didn't know Anna was there. I called 911 and held her until emergency services arrived, then ran outside to flag them down. When I got back to the bedroom, the pistol I kept in the closet lay on the floor near Anna.

"The Reverend blamed me for his daughter's death and used his influence to put me away. And that, my friend, was that. I didn't kill her, but if I had just walked away when her father threatened me, Anna would still be alive."

Miles was quiet for a long time. So long that I began to worry that maybe he didn't believe me. But he finally sighed and somberly said, "I'm sorry, Arthur. They done you so wrong. Both you and your wife. You deserved better."

They took Miles away the next morning. He would get his last meal. His last visitor. And just moments past midnight he would get a one-way ticket to Doreen on the Electric Express.

Three days later, my execution day arrived. Sitting alone in my cell waiting for them to take me, it occurred to me that the odds of my execution day falling so close to Miles's felt like more than coincidence. Fate's strange twist, I supposed.

A guard approached my cell and said I had a visitor, which I found puzzling because I had already said goodbye to my sister and visitation hours had passed. The guard said, however, that this was a special situation. In the corridor outside my cell, a young woman stepped into view. She wore

GLIMMER

a stylish maroon beret that matched her skirt and a simple cream-colored blouse. Her smooth hands, with chewed off fingernails, fiddled nervously with car keys on a VW key chain.

The guard walked away and the light he had blocked flickered across her face. My eyes widened in recognition. I knew her. She had been with Miles on visitor's day. It was his daughter.

"Mr. Aikens?" she asked softly.

"Ye-yes?" I had already forgotten how to speak.

"I'm Nicole Monroe. Miles's daughter."

"Yes. I know who you are. I saw you with Miles on visitor's day. He spoke of you often."

"I just wanted to thank you for being such a good friend to daddy. He often mentioned what a lonely place prison was. He told me that at least he knew before he died that he had made one real friend. Thank you for making those last months of his life more meaningful."

She pulled a handkerchief from her purse and dabbed her eyes. My eyes had teared up, too.

"He had a message he asked me to pass along to you, but I confess I'm not sure what it means."

"Ok," I said calmly, though I found myself oddly nervous.

"He said to tell you that not even angels can be good all the time. Do you know what that means, Mr. Aikens?"

I shook my head. "No, I'm sorry. I don't." But inside I was shaking. How could Miles have known that was how I saw him? Unless...

Miss Monroe sighed, clearly disappointed. "Oh well. Another enigma wrapped in an enigma about daddy."

"What do you mean?" I asked, though I thought I already knew.

"Oh, my father was a strange man. When I was little, he used to take me on these pretend walks all over the world and it was like we were really there. It was like—"

"Magic," I said.

108

GLIMMER

Miss Monroe seemed taken aback. "Why, yes, it was exactly like magic. What made you say that, Mr. Aikens?"

I shrugged but quickly glanced away. "Just a guess."

She eyed me shrewdly. I think she suspected I knew more than I was saying, but let it pass.

"You know my father didn't mean to kill my mother. That night, I tried to calm him, to tell him it would be ok, but I reckon he was having one of his episodes—his Vietnam flashbacks—when he didn't like to be touched. You knew he was a prisoner of war for three years?"

I shook my head. "No. He never said anything about it."

She nodded. "Yeah, the night of the incident, Daddy balled up on the couch and wouldn't calm down. My mother heard the ruckus and came running down the stairs. But I guess Daddy only saw the Viet Cong. When she came to him, he shoved her away, and well... You probably know the rest."

I nodded.

"I'm so sorry, Miss Monroe. I—" I started to say something more—but hesitated.

A flicker of concern crossed her face. "What is it, Mr. Aikens?"

I sighed. "Well, as you mentioned, Miles told me that something had upset him that night before your mother passed, but I didn't want to pry so I never asked what happened."

Miss Monroe hesitated and glanced down the far end of the corridor where the guard stood. She locked eyes with mine and leaned forward, speaking in a low whisper.

"I guess it doesn't much matter now, but Daddy confessed everything to me. He said he had been in a special unit in the war. An Army Ranger Sniper Unit. He had this lieutenant that commanded the unit and, well, after the war, Daddy sometimes still did things for him. About a month before my mother died, Daddy lost his job and was in a real bad place financially. He said the lieutenant always knew things like that and had reached out to him about making some money. He wanted Daddy to scare this man. Some bad guy. The lieutenant told him the man was a child molester. Daddy was only supposed to nick him in the arm. Draw a little blood. He could do that, you know. But turns out, the man's wife was there. And just as he fired, she stepped in front of him and was killed."

I only heard a roar in my ears; a hurricane in my head. How could this be? Not Miles. Not my gentle old friend; my guiding angel.

It barely registered when Miss Monroe said her goodbye and turned to leave. But as she walked away, I heard her say something that brought ice to my veins.

"Well, what do you know? There's the Lieutenant now. Only Daddy said these days he prefers to go by the Reverend. Good afternoon, Reverend. Thank you again for the lawyer you got for Daddy."

"Why, it was nothing, Miss Monroe. Always happy to help my friends. I'm just sorry it didn't turn out better for him."

My head spun. I grabbed hold of the bars on my cell to steady myself. Squeezing my eyes shut, my mind raced to put it all together.

Suddenly, the pieces fit.

Not only had the Reverend manipulated Miles into shooting into my house, an act that killed Anna—his very own daughter, but he then arranged for me to be blamed for her murder and get sentenced to death—with an execution date a mere three days after Miles? And how did Miles end up on death row? Even by the most egregious reading of the facts, Doreen's death had been an accident— one for which Miles should have, at the most, received a ten-year sentence for manslaughter. But he got the death penalty? And the Reverend's personal attorney had been at the helm of both actions. "Dear God," I whispered. I wondered then if the Reverend had arranged for Miles to get captured by the Viet Cong all those years ago? The question seemed to answer itself. Just how long had this monster been destroying people's lives?

"A long time," came a whisper.

I looked up to lock eyes with the Reverend. "How did you get past the guards?"

"Didn't you know? The condemned always get religious counsel if they request it."

I glared at him. "Why did you put me here? You know I didn't kill Anna. And why destroy Miles? What did he ever do to you?"

"You are here because you disobeyed me, Arthur. And I did warn you, did I not? And Miles? Back in Vietnam when we were holed up in the jungle, he used to tell his stories and take the entire platoon on his damned walks. The soldiers loved him for it. And I hated him. And his gift. And his kind."

"His kind? What are you talking about?"

"Anna's mother was like Miles, but she made people dream with her piano. A prodigy, they said. But I knew it was more than that. It was unnatural. So, I snuffed out her light, took her child, and raised it as my own—hoping to learn its secrets. But then you came and stole her from me. So now," he said and glanced down the cellblock where Miss Monroe had exited. "Now, I'll play games with Miles's daughter—because she may not know it yet, but she has the gift, too."

I lunged towards him, sticking my arms between the bars, and grabbed him by his neck. With a pent-up viciousness that bordered on insanity, I slammed his head into the bars—not once, not twice, but three massive times. His forehead shattered. Blood, bone fragments, and brain matter shot out—signaling a death blow.

The Reverend staggered back, shocked, wincing, and trying to blink back the blood that had trickled into his eyes.

For but a moment, I savored the sight of my archenemy's demise.

Until he started laughing.

I watched in horror as the blood in his eyes trickled back

up into his crushed forehead—which sealed and healed itself as if it never happened.

I backed away. "What are you?"

When he next spoke, the very walls of the cell block rumbled. "Words don't exist for what I am."

Terrified, I backed against the cell wall and crossed myself in an involuntary fallback to my Catholic upbringing. When my fingers dropped from my forehead, I caught sight of blood on my fingertips and stopped cold, my eyes widening with realization. It was his blood.

It was then I noticed the front pocket of my shirt weighed down. I reached in and pulled out a key chain—the VW keychain Miss Monroe had been holding earlier. She must have slipped it into my shirt pocket when she leaned in to whisper. But why?

Suddenly, I remembered Miles's penny, and him telling me there was enough of his gift infused in it to allow me to spirit walk. My heart began to race.

I stared at the keychain and the blood on my fingertips, recalling the walk in Fern Valley. We mustn't take any living thing with us on our walks, Miles had said. Take the leaf and the tree would die.

Then I thought of Miss Monroe and what the Reverend had said about her. She may not know it yet, but she has the gift, too. I'd bet that from the way she had clutched the keychain that it had plenty of her gift infused in it as well.

But would it be enough?

Nervously, I began pacing in my cell. Dared I even hope?

"What are you doing?" The Reverend asked.

Our eyes locked and, seeing a flicker of doubt cross his face, I felt the momentum of fate begin to shift. I clutched the VW key chain.

"Six steps forward," I said, beginning to walk. "Three steps across. Six steps back, turn and restart."

Like a galaxy spinning in space, the air in the cell began to churn.

The Reverend shook his head in disbelief. "How are you doing this?"

"Six steps forward, three steps across. Six steps back, turn and restart." I said with increasing intensity.

"Guards!" The Reverend yelled, trying to grab at me through the bars. "Guards!"

I quickened my pace, walking now with feverish vigor, chanting the words over and over. "Six steps forward, three steps across. Six steps back..."

And turning one last time, I locked eyes with the Reverend and whispered, "For Anna."

Then with all the force of my will said, "Turn and Re–"

*

D.A. Steen is a writer, reader, scribbler, and dreamer hailing from the magical hills of northern Alabama. You can find his short stories scattered across the internet and him at his page www.facebook.com/thewriterdasteen. One day he might even update his website: www.dasteen.com.

THE TERMINATOR LINE
David Safford

She lay naked in a small boat, her arms resting against the gunwales while her hands dipped below the cool bath of a lake. Tiny waves rocked her with gentle strokes, swaying like a mother's grasp. Her head lay on a pillow while the sun massaged her young, thin body. Between the crisp water curling around her fingers, and the warm yellow rays from above, the day was perfect. She basked in it without needing to sleep or wake. She simply was.

She took a deep breath, and sighed.

*

The woman awoke with a bestial scream at the sensation of a spear slicing through her kidneys. Her hands flew to her torso, hugging it to somehow quell the pain.

Then something twisted the spear, grinding into her abdomen, and she howled.

When she opened her eyes the world was blurry with salt and cryo-retinal disorientation but she could see through the two-centimeter-thick plexiglass shell into the hibernation quarters.

She wailed and slammed her hands against the moisture-coated surface, then recoiled at the violent fire raging in her belly. Her breath came like the desperate inhalations of the drowning.

Meanwhile, everything inside her was wrapped in

writhing razor wire.

She beat the glass again with her fist. Then she saw movement.

She twisted to her back and pressed against her belly, a massive white globe protruding from her guts. Everything was on fire, the center of the sun.

She screamed as the translucent shell began to rise, the deathly chill of the living quarters throwing her into convulsions and her flesh bursting with goose pimples.

"Hold on!" she heard the man cry. "It's going to be okay!"

No, she thought, shaking uncontrollably. No, it's not.

Then it all vanished. The caldera cooled and the claws were blunted and she suddenly felt nothing more, and everything went black.

*

When she came to he helped her stand and dress and stumble to the mess area for some rehydrated ice cream. She spooned it into her mouth slowly, savoring each spark of sugary delight on her tongue, and stared at the table. In her belly a little flutter told her that the ice cream was appreciated. She smiled weakly. Across the table, the man watched her in silence.

At last she finished her cup and set the titanium bowl and spoon on the table with a clank.

"So," she said, her throat dry, "are we there?"

The man continued to watch her. "We are."

She laughed in seeming relief. "That's wonderful. What's its name again?"

He bowed his head. "Wolf 1061-C."

She frowned at him and repeated, "Wolf 1061-C. What do the sensors tell us?"

The man swallowed, staring into the slate oblivion of the table. "They're still gathering data. What about you?"

He lifted his gaze to meet hers again. His proud eyes

seemed to quiver under his sculpted brow and dark head of curly hair. She shivered at his look.

"I'll be fine."

The man cleared his throat and stood. "And our boy?"

She patted the soccer ball-sized bulge. "You mean, our girl."

He smiled. "Fine," he said, his voice catching a little. "Our girl."

"Whatever you did saved her," the woman said softly.

"Her… and you."

"Thank you."

He rested his hands on the back of his chair. "It's gotten worse every time. I was able to get her heart rate back to normal, but for a moment there…." His voice faded.

She nodded. "I know."

"There's more," he said. "The Medicine is running low. I had to give you a double dose. One for you and one for her," he said, coughing. "I don't know if there's enough left to help you wake up again. Or for the delivery."

She stared at him. "I can handle the delivery myself."

"I know," he said, his eyes falling to the woman's belly. "But I'm worried."

The woman shook her head and smiled. "Don't be."

"I am," he insisted, and jerked his head toward the window. "We're low on supplies and I don't know if this planet is what we're looking for."

She glanced past him. The planet wasn't in view, but it didn't matter. "Why not?" she whispered.

"It's tidally locked," he said.

"We knew that."

"But we didn't know how narrow the terminator line would be."

"How narrow is it?"

"Two? Maybe three?"

"Kilometers?"

The man nodded.

She exhaled carefully, staring into the gray nothingness

GLIMMER

of the living quarters. She licked her lips, and said with great measure, "That could be enough."

"For a human civilization?" the man said, his voice sharpening. "It would never work."

"Most of the habitable planets within reach are tidally locked," she said, her voice quiet to balance that of the man. "We knew that a long time ago and calculated the risks accordingly."

"But we didn't calculate that risk!" he said, throwing an open hand toward her belly.

She gasped in recoil. "She's not a risk."

He collapsed into his chair and rubbed his eyes, his hands trembling. "Proxima... nothing. Teegarden... no atmosphere. Kapteyn, Gliese...." He laid his arms on the table and buried his face. "All of them dead. Lifeless. Hopeless!"

"What about this planet?"

He lifted his head and scoffed. She narrowed her eyes at his childish outburst but he didn't notice, stalking over to the window. "Look at it," he said.

"At what?"

"*It.* This stupid planet."

She stood and shuffled toward him and took his arm. "Show me," she said.

He stepped back to give her the window and she took his place.

It was a mammoth brown eyeball with a pupil of blasted red canyons and an iris of sinuous, cracking valleys. Nearer the perimeter, where the rays of the nearby red dwarf weren't quite so intense, little capillaries of sapphire blood flowed into the shadows beyond the narrow terminator line.

"Do you think there are oceans back there?" she said.

"The sensors do," he said. "But are they sufficient for sustaining life? I doubt it."

"They could be," she said, gazing into the infinitely detailed cracks and crevices of the bronze world.

"Of course they *could,*" he said, his voice darkening. "But readings of the surface give an average temperature on the helio side of one-ten, 'C'."

"One *hundred* ten?"

He nodded, his face reflecting pale in the window. "As for the other side, the sensors can only guess. But right now they're estimating minus twenty-to-thirty."

"Meaning it's frozen."

"Yes."

"What about the habitable zone?"

He snorted. "You mean the string of dirt we'd get to live on?"

"Yes," she said, shooting him a withering glare, "I do."

He sighed. "Currently, at least near the equator," he said, "it's twenty-four degrees."

Her mouth opened, tongue wet. "Twenty-four?"

He nodded. "Yup. At least while this high-pressure system lasts. There's a low front that will blow through in a few hours."

"Twenty-four," she repeated, and closed her eyes.

She could almost feel the soothing heat rubbing her throbbing forehead, and the soft cool waters slipping over her fingertips.

"I don't think it's worth it," the man said, interrupting her fantasy. "If something goes wrong and we need to use the Medicine to survive down there, we can't risk hypersleep again. If we're down to one dose, or worse, we're out, then we'd…"

His words caught in his throat and he swallowed.

"We'd have to make a choice," he said.

A choice.

The baby whirled within her a moment and she lost her balance, stumbling. He lurched forward to catch her, but she steadied herself against the hull. They stood in a silence, eying each other.

"I know you're worried," she said at last. "But we owe it to the people of Earth to at least try."

He scowled. "It's a hopeless, lifeless rock, just like the

others."

She lifted her eyes to his. "Maybe it isn't. Maybe it's our new home."

He touched her middle. "What about her?"

She laid her hand over his, and the child sent a playful kick against their fingers.

"We'll be okay," she said.

*

The lander plummeted toward the surface at an infernal twelve kilometers per second. Engulfed in flames as the heat shield smashed into the thick atmosphere, the man gritted his teeth through a mask of sweat and wiggled a joystick to fire stabilizing jets. Beside him, soaked in an equally thick pool of sweat, the woman squinted at a readout of altitude and descent angle, her fingers dashing over buttons to fire rockets that kept them from nose-diving and burning into ash.

For ten minutes they concentrated on their tasks, wiping moisture from their eyes as atmospheric entry wrapped them in a fiery cone of hell. Then they sliced through a thick mop of clouds and blue light sprayed through the tiny portholes and onto their faces, and they burst into relieved laughter. With a jolt, parachutes jerked them back into their seats to slow the fall even more.

"Go on D-Rockets 1 and 2?" the man said.

"D-Rockets are Go," the woman replied.

With the flick of two switches, they felt another jolt at their backs as the descent thrusters belched into life, pushing against gravity to lower them to the ground.

"This spot looks perfect," the man said, pointing to a digital topographic diagram.

The woman nodded. "Go for landing."

The man flicked another stick and the craft swayed, wobbling in balance from the rockets. A whirring rumble made their teeth chatter. The landing gear had automatically extended.

Then, with a solid boom, the craft moved no more.

The man flicked the same switches back down while the woman entered a sequence on the panel of buttons, and then the engines howled to a thin whine.

They looked at each other.

"We're here," the man said.

*

She triple-checked his pressure suit and oxygen levels before turning so he could check hers. Then, with a heavy grunt, she helped him unlatch the hatch and swing it open. They stepped outside to take in the new world.

She stood on a hard-packed platform of cocoa dirt and emerald grass. Trees with sinewy trunks crept out of the ground, their bushy crowns bent like they were bowing to some great king. Beyond, as far as the eye could see, rivers ran in thousands of glistening purple trenches like the veins of a great giant. A river snuck along the ground not far from their landing site, its waters rippling brilliant reflections of white and yellow into her eyes. And in the midst of it, floating on the glassy surface, she thought for a moment there was a small boat, a woman lying inside of it, her arms trailing beside. Blinking, she saw indeed there was no such thing before her.

"Look," she heard the man say through the comm.

She turned from the stream and walked back to him, noting that the gravity on Wolf 1061-C must be roughly eighty percent of Earth's, or at least what she remembered of Earth's gravity.

"Do you see this?" the man asked, pointing into the distance.

She lifted her eyes.

Not far from where they stood was a distinct line, stretching from north to south. On their side of it, the world seemed normal, lush with blue vegetation and soothing sunlight. But beyond the land faded into a barren, parched desert. The trickling rivers and their scintillating pools vanished into arid ruts and ditches.

She shuddered at the sight of such hell so near. Yet her feet stood upon a vibrant carpet of life, green with grass and blue with water. Something about it filled her with dread, so she turned away, toward the opposing hemisphere.

What she saw there was no less troubling.

First, she could espy nothing. All was a thick fume of darkness. But as her eyes adjusted to the murk, they detected a tumultuous boil of clouds.

"A storm," she whispered.

It was nearly impossible to discern where the rivers led on this side of Wolf 1061-C. Their shades faded to a deep, chilling cobalt nearly as dark as midnight. Surely they froze within a few kilometers of the terminator line. And then what?

She took a long breath that stung with a certain awareness of the truth.

No, she thought as her eyes continued to drink of the distant darkness and its boiling black thunderheads. *This is not humanity's hope.*

Then she felt another whirl in her stomach.

Nor is it ours.

"We should go," she said quietly, "before that storm hits."

The man stood in silence a moment, then put a hand on her shoulder.

"We could ride it out if I got the shelter up," he said, his voice weak. "This place isn't so bad, you know."

He sounds desperate.

"No," she said, closing her eyes. "Humanity could never survive here."

"Yes, it could," he said. "There's water, there's life…. *Complex* life!" His eyes were wide with excitement. "We haven't found anything like that yet. Right?"

"Right, but…."

"I was wrong before," he said, taking both her arms in his gloved hands. "We have nothing to worry about."

She turned back to the scalded plain to their right, and then to the shadowed miasma to their left. The thickening clouds seemed closer now, like a wall of boiling tar charging their way. A tumble in her middle sent a brief wave of nausea up her throat.

"We need to get back to the lander," she said, swallowing.

"Let's set up the habitat," he said. "We can make it work."

"No," she said, and pointed toward the rising darkness. "We have to go."

"Listen!" he cried, placing a hand over the wriggling bulge of her belly. "I'm not going to risk another hypersleep! Do you want this child to live?"

She could barely catch her breath, and whispered, "Yes…."

His eyes blazed, burning with the desperate fire of survival. "Then help me get the shelter up!"

He marched toward the nearby lander, its heat shield still smoking from their arrival. She watched him for a moment, nausea throbbing within her. She doubled over and breathed slowly, in and out, gasping.

She looked up. A shadow had fallen. The storm had swarmed over the light now, its purple-bruise feet trampling the rivers of Wolf 1061-C.

"Wait!" she yelled, beginning to job. "We don't have time. Get in the lander!"

The man didn't respond. She circled the vehicle and found him in the rear, opening the compartment where the inflatable habitant was tucked for flight.

"It's too late. We have to go!"

His hands unsnapped a series of straps tethering the habitant in its compartment.

"We don't have a choice," he muttered. "We're staying."

"We can't!" she cried, grabbing at his hands. "Stop!"

"Hey!" he yelled, swatting her away.

She back-pedaled and suddenly lost her balance, tumbling to the ground. The man whirled to face her.

"Don't you understand?" he bellowed, his face red within his mask. "We have to make this work. There's water. There's life. There's *hope*," he said, nearly breathless.

But under the swelling umbrella of broiling umbra, his words felt like a death sentence. The tears came and flowed over her.

Yet beyond her sobbing there was a growing sound, a white noise that swelled from a hiss into a low roar.

The man stood over her. "I'm sorry!" he cried, reaching out a hand. "Get up and help me!"

The roar spread like a bomb. The air was growing terribly cold. She shivered at a gust of wind yet somehow the man didn't seem to notice. He turned and jerked a strap loose, sending a corner of the deflated habitat tumbling out.

"Get up and help me!" he shouted, reaching for her hand. "It's the only way!"

She wept and the sky soured, soaked with a black deathly veil. Dirt and sand and ice began to whip past them. Dust levitated and swirled like a tornado. The temperature plummeted and her teeth began to chatter uncontrollably despite her climate-controlled suit.

She staggered to her feet. "Inside the lander! Now!"

He turned his back and yanked on the fabric of the habitat. "No!" he replied.

"Get inside now! That's an order!"

The darkness fell deeper and everything vanished. A gust of wind knocked her back and she stumbled, dizzy-drunk, groping in the blind for the door. Her fingers closed on metal and she pulled with all her strength.

"Hurry!" she cried.

Then she heard a scream.

The wind shrieked in fury and the door flew wide against her grip. Clawing at its edge, she hauled her body into the cockpit one centimeter at a time and swung the mighty door

GLIMMER

to a close.

Then she waited for him to appear at the window. For his face to shine through the glass. For his voice to call out to her.

All she heard was the howl of the storm in the impenetrable dark.

*

She found him six hours later, three kilometers from the lander in the sun-scalded desert. His mask was shattered and shards of glass glimmered in the flesh of his face and one of his eyes.

He looked dead. But when she lowered her ear to his mouth, the faintest possible wind of breath greeted her.

A glimmer of hope burst like a firework in her and she set to work.

She'd wisely brought a collapsible stretcher from the med kit and now she rolled him onto it, then began the long hike back, dragging him behind. Sweat poured down her face and her breath fogged up the glass and she collapsed over and over again from the heat, but willed herself back to her feet and kept going.

It took an hour just to lift him into the lander and secure him to his seat. All the while his breathing did not cease, though it was ragged and sick, like his soul was already crying out to God.

She wore no safety straps of her own, as the launch sequence required her to perform the duties of two. The cockpit blasted skyward, leaving the landing gear and cargo hold behind. The fuel burned until the tanks were dry, expending barely enough energy to escape Wolf 1601-C's gravity and send them hurtling back into orbit. She piloted the craft back to their interstellar mothership, docked, and opened the hatch.

She dragged him through the airlock and laid him flat on the floor of the ship. Still, he clung to life, his tiny puffs of breath weaker than before, his flesh cool and rubbery.

She ran to the Med Pod and snatched the container of Medicine. The Medicine was a cocktail of adrenaline and morphine and hormones mixed by the scientists on Earth to deal with the worst medical emergencies imaginable, to bring the near-dead back to life.

It was what the man had had to use on her each time they woke from hypersleep.

Hurrying back to the man's side, she knelt and opened the plastic box and peered inside and yelped in shock.

There were only two syringes.

One for you, he had said.

And one for her.

She held her belly as a tremor shook her entire body. She fell to the floor and wept again. Then she squeezed her middle and imagined the tiny creature within, clinging to life each time they entered the ice, laying down to sleep in an arctic tomb. She thought of its agony, its confusion at the numberless knifepoints of pain as it discovered warmth again, its heart racing in panic and stress and trauma.

Then she thought she felt a kick in response.

My sweet, she called out of her soul.

She took one of the two doses from the case. Then, lifting her eyes to the dying man, she jabbed the needle into his neck and pressed her thumb upon the plunger.

*

The first thing she noticed was the warmth. Like a blanket.

She looked down at her bare, smooth midriff glowing bronze around the sunken cove of her belly button. She drank deep gulps of air and leaned her head back to sleep again.

The water gurgled as the boat rocked, jostling ever-so-softly in the wind and the waves. Her hands swam freely, the cool water running up her wrist to send a soothing breeze up her arms and into her chest.

The boat creaked again, its balance somehow unsure. She opened her eyes, lifted her head, and gasped.

There was a child sitting in the boat.

It was maybe eighteen months old, thick hair curling around its head, its flesh golden in the sunshine. It, too, was naked.

"Hey, sweet girl," she said.

The child turned. It had a face, but it was as in a haunting dream when features are optical illusions and the sleeper feels amnesiac and ready to plummet over some ever-present knife's edge.

She stared at the child, blinking. "Are you my daughter?" she asked finally.

The little creature nodded.

The woman laughed, and extended her hands. "Come," she beckoned, "come to me!"

The child clambered into her lap without a sound, and a new warmth spread over her middle.

There was a sudden jolt against the side of the boat. She looked up and discovered they had reached land, the bottom of the boat sliding over a rich layer of creamy brown mud.

"Are you ready?" the woman asked.

The child slipped its hand into hers.

She rose and helped the child to its wobbly feet.

She knew what was coming. Even in her dream, white-hot pinpricks of pain unspeakable poked at her body. A ghoulish breath of cold rippled over her naked body.

She squeezed the little hand, and urged it forward.

"It's going to be okay," she whispered. "Let's go explore."

The child laughed, and leaped over the edge.

*

GLIMMER

David Safford writes adventure stories that you won't be able to put down. Read his latest story at his website. David is a Language Arts teacher, novelist, blogger, hiker, Legend of Zelda fanatic, puzzle-doer, husband, and father of two awesome children.

Website: http://www.davidsafford.com.

HOPE IN A BOWLING ALLEY
Carole Wolfe

As soon as the bowling ball flew out of his hand, Max Shaw knew it was destined for the gutter. The ball swerved left, then careened right before teetering on the edge of the lane. It hung on a few more inches before dropping into the trough, missing all of the pins.

Shuffling back to the ball return, Max sighed. He'd hoped his retreat to the bowling alley would help him destress from his latest argument with Helene. It had the opposite effect. He was more on edge than when he arrived. And his bowling average was in the toilet.

He looked up at the score. The blinking zero taunted him. Fifth frame and he'd yet to break 100. Maybe he should call it a night. If he kept this up, not only would he still be mad at Helene, but he'd never hear the end of it from his bowling buddies.

Reaching down, he unlaced his bowling shoes as he thought about how unsatisfying his life had become. He hated confrontation so he worked hard to keep the peace with Helene.

It wasn't always like this though. When they were first married, Helene loved everything about him. She was relaxed and down to earth. Nothing bothered her. But after the girls were born, Helene changed. She wanted more. More of what he had no desire to find. He knew the exact moment things took a turn for the worse.

He remembered it like it was yesterday.

GLIMMER

Years ago, when their girls were in middle and high school, the Shaws had been invited to a Memorial Day weekend party at the lakefront home of Carol and Richard Weaver. Sara did gymnastics with Casey Weaver and Helene took self-defense with Carol.

Helene idolized Carol. The woman headed up every fundraiser and charity function in Glen Valley. She'd married into money, something Max learned Helene had aspired, but failed, to do. Carol married Richard, who was food industry royalty (Weaver's Baked Beans led the market on canned goods of all varieties) but she didn't want to be labeled as a gold digger (even though that's what she was). That appealed to Helene because she wanted the same. The problem was Max didn't come from nor did he make a lot of money.

The house overlooked the lake and had its own dock which accommodated five boats (a race boat, two pontoons, a fishing skid and a ski boat complete with all the bells and whistles one needed for barefoot skiing - though why someone would want to barefoot ski was beyond Max), ten jet skis and a built-in bar that served light beer and lemonade. Small cabins surrounded the house, enough for each of the five families invited.

"I hate camping out," Max said when they were driving to the lake.

Helene filed her nails. "It isn't camping. We'll be in a cabin."

"We're close enough we could just drive back and forth each day. Then we could stay in our own home and not have to worry about spending so much time with these people."

"That's the point, Max. The kids can hang out with their friends. Plus I never get to spend time with Carol. Why waste time driving when I can have the entire weekend with her?"

Max kept driving. In his own house, he could eat his own food and not have to have Weaver's beans with every meal. They gave him gas so it would be hard to explain his

129

constant need to get away from the group. Instead, they were stuck in a two-bedroom cabin with rustic wooden walls which were so thin you could hear everything that went on in the bathroom. Max also noticed there was no lock on the door.

That evening at dinner, Richard asked Max if he wanted to join him for an early morning fishing trip. Max knew that meant getting up while it was still dark, far earlier than one should have to while on vacation, but one look at Helene's face gave him his answer.

"Love to," he said.

The next morning, Max clutched the travel mug of hot coffee that Richard presented him as they boarded the boat. It was pitch black but they were well on their way to the middle of the lake to catch the big one. Whatever that was. Richard's designer rain jacket sported fishing lures attached to one arm and a compass on the other. The boat slowed then stopped as Richard consulted his fish finder. They each got their poles ready and after the first cast, Richard asked, "You still in charge over at the engineering firm? I'm looking for a new head of Weaver's pork and beans department and I thought you might fit the bill."

"Overseeing design specs isn't exactly the same as managing food production. Engineers aren't the usual suspects for the food industry."

Richard laughed out loud. "God, I loved that movie! Kevin Spacey before the fall." Richard reeled in his line and cast again. "Can't be that much different than what you do now. It's all about telling people what to do and documenting stuff. You know how much our monthly budget is for the manufacturing department alone?"

Max shook his head even though he knew the number was probably ten times the annual budget of the small engineering firm he headed. It never failed to amaze him how people prioritized money and status over a job well done and personal satisfaction. Weaver was probably one of those guys who didn't give a shit about what he was making

GLIMMER

or selling as long as he turned a profit.

"I'm an engineer," said Max. "I use my education to create things that are useful in society and to give people in this town a job. Not to line the pockets of those who already have enough as it is."

"Oh relax, Max. Helene always says you're a champion for the underdog, and you would still have plenty of time to do that as head of pork and beans. I've got plenty of paper pushers in that office, but I need a leader to keep them moving in the right direction. Helene tells Carol all the time how hard you work. Don't you want to get paid for all that time? This position starts at $100,000 with a bonus structure that will take total comp in the high six figures. It also gets you a membership at the country club so you can treat Helene to a special dinner a couple of times a week. Plus you can bring the family to use this lake house whenever we aren't here. Helene can coordinate with Carol."

"I take it Helene already knows about this?" Max asked.

Richard's fishing line bent and he got busy reeling in a 12-inch bass, which would become an 18-inch one when Richard told the story at dinner that night.

Max stewed about Richard's offer but decided not to bring it up to Helene until they got home. The cabin's walls were so thin the girls would be able to hear them if they argued, and an exchange of words was inevitable.

Helene, of course, had her own agenda. As they were getting ready to walk to the big house for fireworks, hotdogs and more Weaver's Baked Beans, she asked, "What did you and Richard talk about while you were fishing this morning?"

He shrugged. "Fishing stuff. How big his boat is."

Her eyebrows furrowed. "That's it? He didn't mention the opening he has to head the pork and bean department?"

"So you did know about this. Thanks for giving me a heads up."

"Max, we've been through this before. You've got too much potential to be stuck where you are. No one over there appreciates what you do for them. And don't get me started on your salary. Don't they know we have two daughters who need to go to college?"

"I like my job. Working with the guys makes me happy. Last time I checked, we're doing just fine in the money department. Why do we need more money? I thought our lifestyle was pretty good as it is."

"Friday night dates at the Applebee's aren't anything compared to the country club."

"Oh, so this is all about our social status." He pointed at her. "No, your social status. Why can't you be satisfied with who we are? I don't need to be one of this town's up-and-comers. I'm happy where I am."

"There's nothing wrong with wanting more." Helene stuck out her bottom lip. "Just because I want our children to have access to the best education money can buy-"

"Of course, it's going to come back to giving the kids an education at some private Ivy League institution. Last time I checked our public schools are doing just fine. I have a job. You could have one too if you didn't insist on pretending that we're something we're not."

"How dare you speak to me like that?"

Sara walked into the room and folded her arms over her chest.

"Tasha's crying, again. Every time you fight, she thinks you're getting a divorce. Now her face will be all puffy by the time we get to the party." She rolled her eyes before she walked back into the room. "Get over it, you two."

Max shook the memory out of his head as he tucked his shoes into his bag. He walked to the return to pack up his favorite bowling ball, the blue and white fourteen-pound one that Helene custom-ordered for their fifth wedding anniversary. Turning it in his hands, he read the inscription.

"To my knight in shining armour. You saved me! I'll always be grateful. I love you!"

Max closed his eyes as tears threatened to fall. Images of his life with Helene flashed through his mind. The shy, timid girl he met in high school. His excited and nervous bride. The fiercely protective woman who'd given birth to their children. His powerful, confident partner of thirty-plus years.

His love made him forget tonight's argument. He wasn't perfect, nor was Helene. But they'd shared too many good times to give up now.

There was hope for them.

Max hefted the bowling bag over his shoulder and headed to the parking lot. He had some things to fix tonight.

*

Carole Wolfe started telling stories in the third grade and hasn't stopped since. While she no longer illustrates her stories with crayon, Carole still uses her words to help readers escape the daily hiccups of life. Her debut novel, My Best Mistake – Tasha's Story, *follows a single mom as she stumbles through one mishap after another.*

When Carole isn't writing, she is a stay-at-home mom to three busy kiddos, a traveling husband and a dog that thinks she is a cat. Carole enjoys running at a leisurely pace, crocheting baby blankets for others and drinking wine when she can find the time. She and her family live in Texas.

WHEN THE CARNIVAL CAME TO TOWN
Theresa Jacobs

Christopher kept to the back of each ride, sure to stay out of sight of the carneys. Twilight lay a blanket of darkness to the shadows where he hovered. Behind the constant whir, bang, hum, loud rock and roll, along with kids hooting and hollering, he never had to worry about making a sound. Tonight marked his third night sussing out the traveling carnival, and he hoped his last.

Following the Ringmaster was easy as pie. The man had to be near seven-feet tall, he wore black silk pants with a blazing red stripe down the outer leg, and he was never without his top hat. The oddest thing was he was never without sunglasses either, even at night. His attention was drawn from his mission as two teenaged girls, leaning into each other giggling, moved to the counter at the ring toss. He pressed between the concessions, careful not to trip on the thick rubber wires, as he tried to hear what was being said.

"Ah, lovely young ladies!" A short man with greased back hair, too toothy of a grin, and wrinkles for days, winked conspiringly—like they knew the trick to win. "Step up, try your hand and catch a prize!" He pranced around the space inside the booth, gathering plastic rings. "You can win yourselves a cute stuffed unicorn there. Just as pretty as you both." With a wink and smile, he placed the rings in the one girl's hand.

GLIMMER

Even from Christopher's nook he saw the young girl flinch from the carney's touch. Crouching down to his knees, he leaned against the booth, aiming to see the thin, blonde girl's face as she tossed the rings. He hadn't yet been able to sort out how people approached the games normal, laughing, happy, having a grand ole time, only to walk away in a dumb state. As though their heads were empty of self-thought. He had no other thought for it himself, other than *empty*.

The teen's hand rose, the yellow ring left her fingers; it floated across the space, hit a bottle, tinged, bounced and rolled away. The carney gave a low *tsk*, but didn't shout out or entice her to try harder. He was watching her eyes. Even the waiting friend had grown quiet. Around them, lights flashed, danced and sparkled as darkness grew deeper. With the last ring tossed the girls turned, dumb-struck now, and walked away.

Christopher watched them go, then looked back to the ring toss. The carney gathered up the errant rings, returning them to his pouch, and sat. Not needing to see more—he'd already watched the exact same oddity transpire countless times over the last three nights—he moved on. What he needed were answers. What were these guys doing to people? Could he find any authority that wouldn't lock him up and think he was crazy? Was there a way to reverse it? Whatever *it* was?

Four days prior, the carnival had come to his town of Blue Springs. On the night of the family outing, Christopher was feeling under the weather. The other four had traipsed off to enjoy the thrills, take in the junk food, and play games, leaving him behind. But when they came home, his family had changed. They continued to go through the motions of life, but in a quiet, zoned out state. They didn't talk, or interact with each other, or him. He'd yelled at them, he shook them, he even went so far as to punch his older brother in the stomach. Only a short time ago this would have elicited a good beating. But now there was no reaction, not even a raised eyebrow. At any time in the past, he would have said his family was a nuisance, his brothers were mean, his father demanding, and his mom too emotional, he longed for those people back. Now, fighting back tears— no sixteen-year-old guy in his right mind would cry - he blended back into the shadows, searching for the Ringmaster again.

Glancing up and down the midway, looking beyond the naïve marks, past the calling carneys and ignoring the tanned, leggy girls, he spotted a tall shadow disappear into the funhouse. Eye on the prize, he took considerable strides after the man, avoiding people like a pinball down an inlane, when a sandpapery grip jerked him to the right and nearly off his feet.

"Whaa-"

"Where you rushing off to, sonny? You look like a strapping young man. Why not try your hand at the ten-in-one." The carney chewed out his spiel, still holding Christopher's arm while rolling three baseballs in his other mitt of a hand.

For the briefest of moments, he thought, *And what if I did? It's one way to see what happens. I can pull away before my mind gets melted.* He looked into the carney's dark eyes and didn't like what stared back at him. There was something not right about the man. He had no whites to his eyes, at least none that could be discerned in the darkness. They appeared as blind pits of tar.

He pulled back. "Sorry sir, my sister is waiting to go on the teacups. I'm already late." He was surprised at how easily the lie tumbled from his lips.

The carney's nose crinkled oddly and his eyes narrowed as if he was sniffing out the lie. "Just three tosses boy. Ya sis can wait I'm sure."

"Nah, I'm already in good with ma, but thanks for the offer."

As another unsuspecting mark took up the carney's attention, Christopher spun and took off at a light jog. Sweat dripped down his back as the funhouse grew closer. The attraction was set up off the ground in what appeared to be tracker-trailers lined up in rows, with metal stairs leading to a giant, open clown mouth. Turning and looking back at the raucous carnival, this end of the field had an abandoned feel to it. There were no overhead lights. No crazy, pumping music, and it was a good twenty feet or more away from the rest of the games. He checked to ensure no one was watching and hurried into the darkness under the iron stairs.

"What am I doing here?" he asked himself, not for the first time, as he waited to make sure no one was coming after him. After a few minutes on his knees in the grass, he decided what he must do. Go inside the funhouse.

His heart picked up the pace as he moved from under the stairs and tiptoed up them. The large round O of a mouth did not appear fun. The clown's eyes were downcast, staring in a peeling royal blue at all who entered. The lips, once red, had dulled to salmon pink, and he felt like they'd close around him the minute he stepped onto the red-carpet tongue. Knowing that he had to follow through, he gulped and took a fast leap into the attraction.

The door remained open behind him, as he knew in his mind it would, but his clenched sphincter still told him otherwise. The hallway was one person wide and lined with small, round pot lights along the floor. From this angle, they cast long, dancing shadows around him. All the hair on his body stood on end. Despite the heat of the July, chills ran up his spine.

He walked slow and quiet, listening for any sounds from within, and wondered what direction he should take. He had never been in a funhouse before and had no clue what to expect. What was so fun about it anyways? He thought, just as the floor beneath his feet tilted. Stretching out his arms, he teetered like a drunken sailor from side to side, and inadvertently cried out. He braced himself from tumbling over when the floor tipped the other way. The next section was convex and as he stepped down it began to spin beneath

GLIMMER

his feet.

"Shit!" The idea of sneaking in was lost to his unexpected reaction. As he staggered off the rolling barrel, puffs of air shot out with loud, compressed bursts.

He realized that each section was like an obstacle course. Passing the skirt blowing portion, the next ten feet were oddly shaped mirrors. As he moved, they distorted and contorted his features. Seeing himself all misshapen gave him the willies again. "How much more do I have to take?"

He wished he'd waited outside, when he heard loud voices echoing from ahead.

Finally seeing a t-off in the hallways, he paused, listening.

Turning left, he followed the voices to an open room. His heart fluttered again, his stomach churned in knots, and his palms grew cool with sweat. There was nowhere for him to hide and watch. He bent down to his hands and knees, stayed tight to the wall, and crept quiet as a mouse along the hall until he could see partially into the room.

It appeared to be a makeshift office, with a single-person wood desk upon which the Ringmaster half perched. A younger man, his face pale and tight with fear, sat in one of the two worn purple guest chairs, the Ringmaster hovering above him.

"I'mmm sssory, Vasilica I…" the young man stuttered, wringing his hands red in his lap.

"Ssssorry? You sniveling rot! I expect at least two feedings a night. You've been here three months. Three months!" The Ringmaster seethed, hissing through his teeth.

Christopher's heart went out to the guy who appeared to be only a few years older than himself. He looked away as a tear fell from the man's eye, and wondered how long this dressing down had been going on for. But he didn't have to worry because it didn't last much longer.

"Really Vas…no! No! please…"

He looked up to see what was happening just as the Ringmaster was lifting the young man from his chair.

GLIMMER

The man's legs flailed ineffectually against the Ringmaster's shins as he was lifted effortlessly into the air. The Ringmaster's lips pulled back in a wide, face-splitting grin, revealing row after row of tiny, pointed teeth stacked one upon another. With his free hand, he reached up, sliding his dark sunglasses down his nose. The young man writhed side to side, gurgling nonsensical noises but not speaking, or screaming. His own eyes fixated on the Ringmaster's. The young man's bladder let loose and his jeans darkened with wet.

Christopher bit his tongue as he held back a cry of his own. Even from his vantage point, he could see the voluminous round eyes of the Ringmaster, bulging outward as though too big for their sockets. They shone, illuminated from within, and altered colors, akin to a kaleidoscope. They turned from all shades of blue to light brown, to green, to grey, to hazel, to white, to black, to dark brown, to violet, and altered faster and faster.

As the young man went limp in the large man's grip, Christopher couldn't restrain a gurgle of fear from escaping his lips this time.

The Ringmaster's head swiveled to the hallway to spot Christopher, a clear form cowering on the floor. He released the young man, who fell into a catatonic heap on the floor.

Christopher didn't hesitate. He pushed himself up, turned back the way he came and bolted. Praying that the speed of youth was on his side, he dared not look back as he took the turn back into the funhouse. He jolted at the sight of himself when he stepped into the mirrored hallway, then realizing it was his own reflection and pushed on. Before he reached the last mirror, the Ringmaster's reflection melded with Christopher's, creating a grotesque amalgamation of the two.

"What are you?" Christopher screamed as he ran on.

Air puffed at him in the skirt-blowing lane, but it would not slow him. He hit the barrel roll at such a high rate of speed that the barrel barely spun. He had a thought that if he could turn his foot as he hit the end, he could get it spinning, slowing the Ringmaster down. But that was a childish thought, there was no time for any tricks. The man, or beast, or demon—whatever the Ringmaster was—with his crazy long legs would be on Christopher before he could hit the outside. And sure enough, as he entered the tilting hallway, the Ringmaster came right behind.

As he tilted right, the weight of the other man began the tilt left, jarring him across the short hall and bouncing him into the left wall. Now with both their weight holding the floor down, they were rammed up on an angle.

"Hold up, stop," a deep voice called out. Multiple forms darkened the hallway.

Christopher's legs gave out, and he fell forward, landing pinched between the wall and the tilted floor. His breath came in short hyper gasps, his heart pounding like a snare drum in his chest.

The Ringmaster shuffled up to Christopher's feet. "How'd he get in here? Get him up. To my place, now," he ordered.

Whether from extreme fear or plain exhaustion, Christopher didn't have time to ponder as he passed out cold.

*

In the darkness under Christopher's eyelids, he imagined he was curled in his bed, dreading the new day. As he moved to stretch out, his length was impeded with a clang. Only then was he aware of being balled up in a small space. Suddenly recalling he'd been captured by the Ringmaster at the carnival, his eyes flew open.

"Well, it lives," Vasilica chuckled.

Christopher gasped, taking in his predicament. He was locked in a cage that might be large enough for a Rottweiler, but certainly not large enough for him. He pressed against the back of the cage, stretching his legs out as straight as he could to relieve the cramping. He said nothing, only glanced warily from carney to carney. Four of them surrounded him, and he avoided the alien gaze of the Ringmaster.

Vasilica leaned over the open wire cage, plucking at the bars as a musician to a guitar. "And just how long were you following us, boy?" he cooed in a soft eerie voice.

Christopher stared at the cage door, already trying to sort out an escape rather than give in to the intimidation of the creeper.

"Oh." Vasilica straightened, holding his excessively long arms out to his sides. "We caught ourselves a toughie here, fellas. Why, just look at him concentrating on that lock." His lips peeled back revealing his pointed, glistening rows of teeth. Moving faster than his large frame should allow, the Ringmaster darted back over the top of the cage. Now above Christopher's head, Vasilica's hot, fetid breath washed over the boy's downturned face. "Well then, perhaps this will entice you to talk."

He spun, grabbed the arm of the carney that had mesmerized the two girls at the ring toss earlier and brought him closer to the cage.

He didn't want to look, but curiosity was his Achilles' heel. Then he wished he'd never come to this infernal carnival. He wished he'd stayed home with his placid zombie-esque family and did his own thing. He could have too. He could have quit school and lazed around the house all day. He could have had any life he wanted.

The Ringmaster tore open the carney's plaid shirt, revealing a horror worse than the sights Christopher had seen as of yet. The man's stomach, although there was no possible way this thing was a man, was a cavern that traveled to a distance farther than human eyesight. The gaping hole roiled blood red with countless souls trapped and screaming inside.

He could not look away even though his mind was

screaming at him to. He watched as people clawed at the opening, their screams echoing around the room, their faces and sex undiscernible. He pissed his pants, then leaned forward and vomited between his legs.

The Ringmaster closed the carney's shirt. He knelt before the cage. "Look at me."

Christopher looked up and stared into the eyes that shifted colors. As a soft blue rose to the surface, he knew they were his mother's, they blended to black, and she was gone. Tears formed in his own eyes and he began to cry in earnest, whether from hunger, exhaustion, or pure terror, he no longer cared.

"You have a choice here, boy. You can be fed to Ungunnolth here and live eternally in that hell. Believe it or not, the souls I eat, while tormented, are not as much so as those are." Vasilica clicked his teeth and waggled his tongue.

The rest of the room remained silent, either they knew not to interrupt the Ringmaster, or they were eagerly waiting for a bite of Christopher.

The Ringmaster resumed, "We always need regular men like yourself to run some of the rides. As you saw, I had to dispose of one such boy earlier."

Christopher gulped and nodded. "H-h-h," he stuttered, cleared his throat and tried again. "How do I take the souls from the marks?"

Vasilica tossed his head back, a deep, rumbling laugh erupting from his gut. His chest rose and fell, causing the silver buttons on his vest to flash blindingly. Then, just as abruptly, his laughter ended and he leaned close to the bars, his teeth bared in warning. "This is the real-world, boy. Not some fantasy novel, or action flick on the big screen. You will work for me behind a booth. You'll eat and sleep in this cage! You'll be my slave until you get old and feeble. Or anger me and I eat you. No hero is going to ride in and save you." Vasilica angled his head, so one eye bulged its prismatic dance at Christopher. "You're still young enough to believe in tripe. But guess what buddy boy, we've been

GLIMMER

doing this carnival for thousands of years."

Christopher began crying again. His eyes darted from man to man—or demon to demon. He didn't know what they were, but they weren't men. He knew the Ringmaster was right, he was too inexperienced in life to know anything. He was surprised that he'd gotten as far as he had without being caught. Now his life, if it would be a life, was in the hands of evil. He had no options. "Yes, sir," he mumbled.

Vasilica clapped and stood. "Ah, I knew you'd choose my way over the tortured soul highway. Tomorrow's a big day, we tear down and move to a new spot. Sleep." He finished leading his troupe out the door, flicking off the lights as he went.

Plunged into darkness, Christopher pulled his legs up to his chest away from the vomit. "What am I going to do? I can't work for him. I just can't." He broke down and cried harder. When the tears dried up, he tried shifting to a better position and felt his belt buckle dig into his stomach. As he pulled to loosen it, the tine jabbed his finger.

"Ohh," he gasped, as a thought came to him. He wriggled around painfully as the cage bars dug into his back and butt. With little elbow room, he unlatched the buckle, yanking the belt out of the loops. Belt in hand he squirmed, maneuvering himself to turn around. He knew the cage was backed up to a wall, now he could only hope it was near an outlet. He had to squint and focus his eyes up close in the dark. At least the walls were white, and that helped to pick up shapes. He made out a dark cord, draped from an end table a mere two feet from him.

Now he had to figure out how to shift the cage. The bars were already killing his knees, but he had to try. Pressing himself as far right as he could, he bounced up. The cage rattled louder than he expected and his breath caught as his heart leaped into his throat. He sat, holding his breath for the count of ten, then waited silently ten seconds more. When no one came bolting through the door, he bounced again, and again, and again. The cage moved a few inches at

143

a time. But it was moving. This gave him hope. He paused to rest, but not too long, and began bouncing again.

Eventually, the cage butted up to the plug in the wall. He reached through the bars, feeling the outlet with his fingers. Sure enough, the only thing plugged in was a single lamp. The bottom was clear.

Not wanting to lose where the outlet was in the dark, Christopher prayed this would work. Taking his belt in hand, he held the buckle tight and pressed the tine between his thumb and index finger.

"I'm sorry, mom and dad. I thought I could save you somehow. I hope someday, someone smarter and braver than me can. I love you."

He hocked a wad of warm spittle on the belt prong and his fingers. Gripping the bars tight with his left hand, Christopher leaned his forehead against the cage. Using his free fingers, he felt for the plug, then below it, the receptacle. Thinking 'god, I hope this works,' he rammed the wet metal tine into the open socket.

*

Outside the huddle of carney trailers, one of the electrical poles sparked a flash of blinding white-blue, popping the transformer. All the trailers whirred to silence as they lost power. If anyone had been looking at the Ringmaster's trailer at that exact moment, they would have seen the inside light up orange as the interior caught fire.

But at that moment, everyone was busy shutting down the midway for the night. They didn't suspect anything until plumes of acrid, poison filled smoke billowed towards the moon. Everyone, including the demon-kind, rushed forward with fire extinguishers.

The Ringmaster's trailer was lost to the fire, all other trailers survived.

GLIMMER

The next morning when the ashes cooled, the Ringmaster pulled a still hot belt buckle from outside the locked, melted cage.

Vasilica tipped his hat to the pile of blackened bones and gave a bow to his first ever escapee.

*

THREE POEMS

Theresa Jacobs

Indie Kin

In isolation I wrote, uncertainty my muse
Pages weighted my days, years evaporated in detachment
Too soon the grave comes to loom, aspirations ached
pursuing
I championed
A hesitant leap from seclusion, my heart grew enlivened
In awe I unearthed my kindred
Ink in our veins, words rattling our brains
United we gather strength
All I ever needed was my indie kin

Happy no matter what

When my heart is broken and the world's got me down.
When the bills pile up and the cash isn't flowing.
When the rain is pouring and I feel like I'm drowning.
I'm not gonna give in and let the sadness win.

I'm gonna crank up the music
I'm gonna shake these blues away.
I'm gonna move.
I'm gonna dance.
I'm gonna take control of my life…today.

When it's Monday and the job is calling.
When it's winter and snow won't stop falling.
When the night comes and loneliness sets in.
I'm not gonna give in and let sadness win.

I'm gonna crank up the music

GLIMMER

I'm gonna shake these blues away.
I'm gonna move.
I'm gonna dance.
I'm gonna take control of my life...today.

There will always be ups and downs.
Someone that may turn from friend to foe.
A pain in your body that just won't go.
But you don't have to give in and let sadness win.
Crank up the music and dance.
You take control...today.

*

Theresa Jacobs believes in magic, fairies, dragons, and ghosts. Yet she trusts science and thinks that aliens know way too much.
Though she still works 9-5 for the man, she has published a horror novel, two Sci-Fi novels, three horror novellas, many anthologies, children's books, and poetry. She is also an ex-contributor to 1428elm.com an online horror magazine.

THE RAINED-ON REINDEER
John King

Wing hated seeing life as so hopeless. She was the kind of girl who wanted to see the brighter side; to look at a storm cloud, and find the silver lining.

But as she trudged into the storm, she could only see black and gray in her path. Her hoodie was pulled low over her face, concealing her dark skin and green eyes. Her freckles were soaked from rain and her own tears.

She had long left the funeral behind, but she could still see the faces of his friends and family. The people she had thought could be the family she had never had. But in their eyes, she saw none of the love and loyalty that had been there in the week before their ill-fated adventure. In its place, she saw the exact same thing:

Why did you have to live and not him? Why couldn't you protect him? Why couldn't you save him?

It was true. She had been responsible for her lover. Where usually, he had reined in her wild and adventurous side, for once, he had treated her and let her lead him on a grand hiking trip into the untamed wild. And what had she done with the new responsibility?

You got him killed, a voice like his mother hissed in her mind. *If you didn't provoke that wolf pack, he'd still be here. It's all your fault!*

Wing's fists clenched in her pockets, begging to be unleashed on something. A post, a mugger, her own face, just something. The one man that had ever shown actual

GLIMMER

care for her - the one that had taken the place of a father that didn't want her - and she got him killed. Physical pain would be nothing compared to the emotional dagger in her heart right now.

No wonder my dad didn't want me, Wing thought. *Connors... Gah, why does it hurt to even say his name?*

Because now he's the perfect poster boy for the 'Stay away from Winifred Nyx' Club, the voice like his mother said darkly.

Wing hunched her shoulders. The rain pattered down, cool and soothing. Even though she wished the rain could be stinging and hard-hitting hail.

In her wandering, she had ended up in front of an out-of-the-way tavern, if it could be called that. The whole thing looked beaten down, like God, Zeus and whoever else ran the world had been using it for a doormat. The roof was built low, like a bunker, and the wood was chipping away in places. A small sign creaked sadly in the wind, displaying a deer with its head bowed. Above and below it were the words 'The Rained-On Reindeer.'

Strangely, she felt as if she had seen this bar before. But the exact memory was failing her.

"Hey," a voice said. Not loud, but soft. Like it didn't care if it was heard or not.

But Wing did hear. Anything to get away from the metaphorical black hole that seemed to have formed in her stomach. Wing saw it had come from an Asian woman leaning against the open door. Her earlobes looked like someone had torn earrings out of them — no blood, thankfully — and her glacier blue eyes radiated bitterness. The sleeveless t-shirt she wore was a bright tie-dye of brown and yellow stains; like people spent their time splashing her with cocktails.

"Bad day?" the woman asked.

Wing shrugged. "Could've been better," she replied. She glanced down at her hoodie. "It's, uh... apparently bad manners to show up at a funeral without a suit. Even if you don't technically *have* a suit."

She wasn't lying. The hoodie was easily the best thing she had – at the very least, it was the cleanest. Yet the rest of Connors' family had stared at her like she had just yanked open the casket and slapped Connors' corpse. It wasn't like they had provided Wing with anything either. They just glared at her until she got the message and slipped out.

Wing nearly got too caught up in her bitter memory, and missed the woman nodding. But she didn't miss her voice.

"Why not get out of the rain, at least?" the woman offered, pushing her door further open. "Get something warm?"

The inside did look warmer than outside. It strangely had a more fluorescent white glow than the normal golden glow she usually saw from lighted houses. But, she didn't exactly have anything better to do. And the woman did sound sympathetic.

So, with a grateful nod, Wing stepped up and into the tavern. Instead of warm air, an A/C unit blasted Wing with a cool air that froze the rain to her hoodie.

Inside, Wing saw around a dozen people, all scattered throughout the bar. None of them had food, but a couple of them had drinks. Most of them were older than her, but she did spot one that looked around her age. A red-haired beauty with a blazer that clung to a really nice back.

Wing huffed. She still remembered how shocked Connors had looked when he caught her ogling girls.

Just cuz I like guys, doesn't mean I can't appreciate girls, too? Wing had asked. *Everything's got beauty to it. Everything and everyone.*

Wasn't as amusing when his mother found out, and nearly had Connors break up with Wing on the spot. Only thing that had calmed the witch down was Wing vowing she'd never touch someone that wasn't her absolutely, positively male son.

But I'm not looking for that, Wing thought as she slid into the seat next to the girl. *Can't girls still be friends with each other too?*

GLIMMER

"Lot of stools in this place," the red-haired girl commented, her eyes focused on a Bloody Mary before her. Wing faltered; the girl's voice didn't exactly imply a want for conversation.

"But only one next to you," Wing replied with a small grin. The girl didn't even look at her.

"I could feel your eyes on my back the second you walked in," the girl said morosely. "And I'm not interested." She shooed at her. "Go find some other kid to seduce, gold-digger."

Whoa, so much for friends, Wing thought, scooting two stools away from the girl.

"I wasn't looking for that," Wing tried to say, but the girl laughed.

"Can you spare me," the girl asked. "People don't care about anything but themselves, and it's pathetic when they try to trick me into believing otherwise."

Cheese and Tap-dancing Crime! Wing thought, putting three stools between her and the girl. *What did I walk into there?*

The Asian woman walked behind the bar, shooting her a smile. Yet, her smile didn't feel genuine. It looked more like the smile you'd get from someone secretly seething with hatred for the entire human race and wishing they could watch the whole planet burn. Wing had worked in enough retail stores. She knew that look well.

"I'd say don't get too mad at her," the bartender said with a shrug. "But... eh, who cares? I've already been blamed for more than enough bar fights. What's one more?"

Wing turned her eyes to the woman. "You were... blamed?" she asked.

The bartender hummed. "I'm at this stupid place every day," she grumbled. "Something goes wrong? It's automatically my fault." She glowered at the liquor glasses like they had done her a personal wrong. "This place already took my dreams, my time, and my dignity. What else could it take?"

151

Wing scooted back. "Can't you do something about it?" she asked. "File a complaint. Ask for time off or something?"

The bartender peered at her, sizing her up and down. She then burst into laughter.

Wing chuckled nervously. Normally, she liked making people laugh, but this laughter wasn't gleeful or full of life. It was when there was nothing else to laugh about but how much life sucked. It made her guts squirm.

"Listen, kid," the bartender said. "You're clearly new here." She took in Wing's dark skin and freckles again. "Lucky for you, I know just the guy to get you up to speed on how the world works." She turned. "DAWN!"

Dawn? Wing thought, before she felt her skin pale. *Oh, no… was that why this place felt familiar?*

In the furthest corner of the tavern, she saw him look up. She saw his freckled face, so much like hers.

"No…" they both whimpered, before Dawn put his head down.

The bartender just chuckled. She shooed Wing towards him with a nod. "Go on, kid," she said. "See where hope gets ya."

Wing's eyes darted between the man in the corner and the bartender, but with another shove, she was sent towards the man. With a broken sigh, the man looked up at her. His eyes weren't green, like hers. They were brown, like a kicked puppy.

"Um…" Wing clenched at her hands. "Hi?"

The man regarded her with those sad eyes. "Hello," he finally replied.

Glancing around at the tavern, she nervously eased into the seat opposite him.

"Um… so…" she stammered. "Dawn, right?" She rose an eyebrow. "You recognize me at all?"

He nodded solemnly. "Winifred Nyx," he replied. "Or, I've heard you go by Wing now?" He glanced at her back. "Despite the lack of wings."

GLIMMER

"It's a lot better than Winifred," she replied, her eyes narrowing at him.

"Eh, call yourself whatever you want," he replied, eyes on his drink. "Might as well call me 'deadbeat' while you're at it."

Wing scooted back in her seat. "Dude," she mumbled. "What is with the negativity here?"

Dawn looked up at her. "The real world," he replied morosely. "Life is misery, and the world is pain." He looked around, before his eyes settled on the bartender. "Michelle hasn't had a vacation day in years." He looked at the girl with the Bloody Mary. "Kira over there gave her heart to someone... and it got stomped on with stiletto heels." He gazed sadly back at Wing. "And me?" he gave a bitter laugh. "I deserve to suffer."

Her eyes twitched. "Why?" was all she could stammer out.

Dawn laughed bitterly. "You need to ask that?" he asked. "I'm a failure." He looked up at her with those kicked puppy eyes. "Look, let's stop dancing around the obvious, eh? You were the only good thing I ever gave this world... and I just wasn't good enough for you."

Wing shifted in her seat, anger starting to replace the shock.

"And you can't even try?" she asked. leaning forward. "Even when I'm right in front of you?"

He shook his head. "What's the use?" he bemoaned. "I'll never be good enough. The child protective service said so. I can't ever be a good enough father for you." He avoided her gaze. "There's just no point. It's all hopeless."

Wing pursed her lips. She had long thought of how she'd confront this man. Thoughts of screaming, or giving speeches, or even just walking out the door. She had considered them all. Yet she had never considered a situation like this; trying to confront a deadbeat who already hated himself. She was going to have to try something different to really get his attention.

153

So, she rose.

"Do you like BDSM?" she asked.

Dawn paused. He looked up at her again. "Do I like what?" he asked.

"You a masochist?" she asked. She glanced around the room. "Do all of you just enjoy being tortured in your spare time?"

"Don't got spare time," Michelle grumped from her bar.

"Well, you could've fooled me!" Wing snapped. She glared around as eyes started to land on her.

"Look, life does suck," she said. "I know that. God, I just came here from my boyfriend's funeral."

Dawn stared up at her in shock, and several people flinched in sympathy.

"But I don't think he'd want me to be miserable without him," Wing insisted. "I think he'd want me to be able to find something happy in life. Even without him."

"Then he hid who he really was from you," Kira replied.

"If that's what you think," Wing said darkly. "You're entitled to your opinion. But I think it's wrong." She looked around. "I think this is all wrong!"

Kira rose with a growl, but Wing strode to meet her.

"You all sit here," she snapped. "Drowning in sorrow and hopelessness, yet you don't seem to want to do a single thing to try and get out of it!" She pointed at Kira. "Some jerk broke your heart? Don't let them win. Find someone else!" She turned to Michelle. "You hate your job? Find another one!" She spun to Dawn. "And you?!" She strode back to him. "If you're so sad about me hating you, how about you actually try talking to me, and changing my – admittedly low – opinion of you?"

Everyone was either staring at Wing, or looking away at their drinks. Wing sighed.

"You all want to say that there's no hope," she said. "And… you're right. There is no hope. Not when you don't want it. Hope is something you have to make for yourselves. Something you earn by looking at the worst life has to offer, and finding something that's still good about it. Something that's worth fighting for."

Wing strode over the door and banged it open.

"And I don't know if it's out there," Wing admitted. "But I'm willing to try and find it!"

She walked out. The rain once again poured on her face, but no longer did she wish that it would sting and hurt. The angry faces of Connors' family couldn't beat her down anymore. And while she still missed her lover, she refused to let the loss of him destroy her. Wing looked back at the way she had come, and she saw the sun's light fighting valiantly against the line of storm clouds.

Wing took a deep breath, and started to walk for the sunlight.

"Wing!" a voice called.

She turned as Dawn stumbled out.

"Can..." he swallowed nervously. "Can I walk you home?"

She smiled softly, and offered her hand.

*

John King is an aspiring novelist and writer. While currently working two jobs in retail, Mr. King hopes to one day turn his simple writing hobby into either a career or a fantasy series that will entertain the masses. He is armed with a Full Sail University Bachelor's Degree in Creative Writing and certification in Microsoft Word, PowerPoint and Publisher.

He has a passion for character writing, and has a fondness for Science Fiction or Fantasy series where all the characters are part of the same universe. Mr. King can be contacted through johnnk1996@aol.com or on LinkedIn at this address: https://www.linkedin.com/in/john-king-9a57b6138/

A CRACK IN THE SIDEWALK
M Mackinnon

What came first—the chicken or the egg? The misery or the rejection? Did he leave because you were a drain on his happiness? Did you lose your children because you neglected them, immured in a morass of self-pity? Did you lose your job because you didn't smile enough? Who knew? Whatever the answer, it had led to this moment, this last lonely walk to the liquor store.

There was a crack in the sidewalk. Crooked and obscene, a disfiguring gash in the cement. Tufts of unwelcome grass poked up from the crack, and ants scurried in and out as if in a hurry to disappear from a world that would allow such ugliness. It spoke of apathy, of impotence, of man's inability to fend off the encroaching wretchedness that was life.

The woman shook her head. It was just a crack, nothing more. The wretchedness was hers alone, the ugliness in her own mind. She was like the ants—running desperately back and forth with nowhere to go, trapped in an existence over which they had no control.

She had something the ants did not, though. She had the means and the will to end it, to stop the ceaseless thoughts that ran through her mind like ice water that trickled down to lodge in her frozen heart. She had the means and the right to stop this nightmare, to end things when they could not get worse.

She stepped over the crack, careful not to disturb the ants, and stood for a moment staring at the doorway before her. Happytime Liquors, the sign above the door proclaimed, its neon light promising comfort and escape from relentless memory. A Shangri-La for the weary traveler seeking safe harbor from a cruel world. An illusion, of course, but one that could be forgiven under the circumstances.

It was a temporary fix, she knew that much. A lie like all the others. It would last only as long as the beautiful bronze liquid in the bottle, and the false warmth in her heart would be gone, leaving the familiar numb feeling that had dogged her for - how long? - was it weeks, months...forever?

Depression is like that, she thought. An insidious, creeping thing. A small disappointment, a tiny resentment, a burgeoning sadness. And then one day you wake up to find that this is your life now—a perpetual dark cloud of misery that lifts only long enough to give a glimpse into how it might have been.

So--the chicken or the egg? Had she always been unhappy, or had life made her so? She couldn't remember. She'd worn a mask for so long it had become glued to her face. Had he seen behind the mask and been repulsed? Was it her fault he'd become cold, stopped loving her, finally left her for a woman who knew how to smile? Did it even matter now?

She sighed. No, it didn't matter. Nothing mattered except that lovely bottle of consolation. It would be her last gift to herself, and when it was gone, she would go too. Just another statistic, forgotten by those who had promised never to leave her side.

"I love you so much," he had said, long ago. "I'm nothing without you." "You're so beautiful." Words. Once she had believed them, but she knew better now. She had never been worthy of such words.

She caught an image in the window of the liquor store's door, and recoiled. Who was that harridan with the lank, greasy hair falling over her shoulders and into her face? What were those dark circles under faded blue eyes sunken

GLIMMER

in a spider web of red?

She stared at pajama bottoms that pinched chubby thighs and puddled onto flip-flops suffocating under puffy feet. A torn plaid shirt clung to every roll as if straining to escape the strangling flannel. Two buttons were missing, allowing a stained white tee shirt to gape.

The woman snorted in disgust. This person looked like something escaped from a defunct circus. Was this the kind of clientele that shopped in her favorite store now? The neighborhood was definitely going downhill.

Bile rose into her throat as she recognized the image. She glared at it with bitter hatred before pushing open the door to head for the bourbon section. Prices had gone up again, which meant she'd be buying the cheapest brand on the shelf. It didn't matter; this was the last time she'd be in this store, and taste was the least of her concerns. A surge of relief rose to mingle with the disgust.

At the counter, she stopped at a display of gift bags. One, decorated like a man's tuxedo complete with a polka-dotted bow tie, seemed to call to her, its whimsy a sharp contrast to the gray reality of her life. Well, this occasion deserved something more than the usual paper bag, didn't it?

She laughed, a sharp, jagged sound. The young clerk looked up from his cellphone and blinked. She gave him her haughtiest smile, and he shrugged and returned to his texting. The woman reached for her wallet and counted her meager collection of bills. Just enough. She slapped the bag down next to the bottle of bourbon, and said, "It's a gift."

"Yeah, whatever." The clerk rolled his eyes and rang up the sale. "Do you want it in the bag, then?"

"Yes, please."

For a moment, it seemed as if the clouds surrounding her had lifted. Her interaction with the store clerk, brief as it had been, was a triumph of sorts. She had been in charge; she'd wanted something and gotten it. They'd had a conversation. She'd almost forgotten what that was like.

By the time she reached the sidewalk, the cloud was

back. A conversation? Who was she kidding? It was the only human contact she'd had in days, and she had been grateful to be sneered at. How pathetic she had become.

Fatigue stole her breath, and she stumbled and braced a hand against the dirty wall of the liquor store. With an effort, she straightened and took the few hesitant steps to a dilapidated bench in the small patch of grass next to the liquor store. There was a pile of old clothes on one end of the bench, but plenty of room for her. She lowered herself carefully to the hard wooden seat and sat for a moment staring out at the street.

She reached into the pocket of her flannel shirt and closed her fingers around a small plastic bottle. It was nearly full, the product of months of cajoling the doctor, telling him she couldn't sleep, that the depression meds weren't working, reducing herself to begging. But she'd gotten them, hadn't she? She'd hoarded them, waiting for the right time.

"Yes," she said out loud. "This is the only way. It'll be over. All of it." She heard a note of desperation in the words—knew they sounded loud and defensive. She repeated them until they sounded right, echoing into the darkness and disappearing. "This is the only way. It'll be over."

"Why are you so loud?" A cracked voice wheezed from the end of the bench. "Can't you see someone's trying to sleep here?"

The woman jerked in surprise, and turned in the direction of the sound. The pile of old clothes rose up, resolving itself into the bent figure of a very old man. Layers of cloth hung from a skeletal frame, and a dirty finger reached up to scratch a gray streaked beard. Sharp beady eyes glinted in the light of the neon sign above the liquor store, reflecting every color in the spectrum.

"S-sorry."

"I don't need you to be sorry—I need you to be quiet." The voice sounded exasperated.

GLIMMER

"I'll go." She struggled to regain her feet.

"Nah, I'm awake now." The old man stared unblinking at her for a long moment. Then he shook his head and turned away, as if the sight of her disgusted him.

She sank back into the hard bench and studied her odd companion. Who was he to judge? His wrinkled visage resembled a crumpled map, the kind her dad had used when they'd gotten lost on vacation, long before GPS had taken the mystery out of a road trip. The old man looked at his lap and plucked at a fold in the rags. He smelled like weeks old garbage.

"Who are you to—?"

The old man turned to her again. Then he smiled, an impossibly sweet smile in a dried-apple face. The missing teeth for some reason did nothing to dampen the charm of that smile, and against her will the woman felt her face crack in response

The grin disappeared.

"What will?" he said.

"Wh—what?"

"What will be over?" The little bird eyes locked onto hers.

A flush rose in her face. "Oh...I was just talking to myself. I—I didn't realize you were there."

"Why is it the only way?" The voice sounded curious, as if she were a puzzle to be solved. The head cocked to one side, making him look like a bedraggled robin eyeing a worm. The woman shivered.

"I-I—"

"You talk a lot, but you don't say much," the old man said. "What will be over? Why is it the only way?" The cracked voice sounded patient, as if its owner was willing to wait as long as necessary for an answer.

Fight or flight, she thought, and straightened her spine. What does it matter now?

"Life. Life will be over." She faced her questioner defiantly.

160

He merely blinked at her. The skeletal fingers rose again, to scratch the thinning gray hair.

"Why?" he asked again, after a moment.

"Because I'm tired," she began.

"So, take a nap."

"It's not that!" Suddenly she was furious. "Are you stupid? My life is more painful than you could ever imagine. I have no one, and no one wants me. Look at me! I'm ugly, and useless. I'm alone in this world, and I hate myself. I have no purpose and I don't even care anymore! I just want to die!" She felt the tears welling, and let them go. Her tears knew the pathway down her face by now.

"Ahh." The old man sat staring out at the street for a moment. When he spoke, his voice was soft.

"Did you know, every sentence you just said began with 'I'? Isn't that interesting?"

She blinked. "So?"

He turned and looked at her again, and then pointed.

"Do you see that crack in the sidewalk?"

Was this old man crazy? Why was she wasting time listening to his nonsense, anyway? She opened her mouth, and then shut it again. Why? Maybe because he was the only human being who had really talked to her in as long as she could remember. People talked at her, but this old goat was actually talking to her. As if he were interested in her answers. She focused on his question, curious for the first time. Would it hurt to be honest, at this point?

"Yes, I see it. It's ugly. Like me. That's probably why I noticed."

"Is it? Ugly?"

"Look at the weeds growing out of it. And those disgusting ants, just running aimlessly in and out. It ruins the sidewalk."

"Are you sure about that?" The hoarse voice was low.

Her head jerked. Her brow furrowed and her breath caught in her throat. She felt something welling up, hot and raw—a new feeling, one she had almost forgotten.

GLIMMER

Emotion. She was feeling emotional—she, who cared about nothing. She cleared her throat and struggled for words.

"Th-that crack is my life. I've ruined everything around me...I'm like those ants, without purpose or meaning, just going through the motions."

"Why do you think that?"

"If someone steps on an ant, no one cares. When I'm gone, no one will notice. Wouldn't it be better if someone repaired that crack and got rid of the ants and the weeds?"

The old man sighed. He scratched at his armpit for a moment, studying the crack in the sidewalk. When he spoke, his words were so soft the woman had to strain to hear them.

"When it rains, water runs into that crack, and then moves through the earth below to sustain life. The weeds are proof of that."

"So?"

"Don't you know anything about ants?" There was derision in the soft tone, she was sure of it.

"Ants don't run about with no purpose. They work together toward a goal. Not a single ant knows the word 'I'. When an ant is crushed under someone's foot, another steps up to take its place. Thus the circle of life continues. No ant is useless, and none are forgotten."

The old man's head snapped up, and now there was anger in the gaze he directed at her.

"Are you lower than an ant? Do you think ants don't mourn when one of them is lost?" He expelled a breath. "Do you think they never wonder why they do what they do?"

"B—but...

"Why are you so different?"

"What?" She recoiled. "I'm not! But the world has given up on me. No one will miss me when I'm gone!"

"Really? You're a part of the world. That means you have a purpose, doesn't it?"

"No, I…"

"How dare you take yourself out of the circle!" The old man's voice was no longer soft; it thundered into the darkness, all signs of age gone. "What will happen if the crack that is your life is sealed up? Why are you so selfish?"

The old man pushed himself up and stood glowering at her. His voice lowered again.

"There's work for you in this world, if you have the courage of an ant. If you can take your place in the crack. Never forget it."

Without another word, the old man turned and walked away from the bench, careful to step over the crack as he shuffled off.

She stared after him for a long time, lost in her thoughts. Then, she reached into her pocket and took out the bottle of pills she had saved for so long. She stared at the label, then opened the bottle and dumped the pills into the grass under the bench.

With shaking hands, she took the bottle of bourbon out of its gift bag and opened it. She clutched the familiar shape of the bottle to her chest and inhaled its heavenly fumes. Then she took a shuddering breath and poured the liquor over the pills at her feet. As she watched, fascinated, the tablets dissolved in the liquid and disappeared into the ground.

In a panic, she fell to her knees in the grass. She scrabbled at the wet mess, trying to close her hands around the disappearing pills, but they were gone, melted into the ground as if they'd never been.

With a choked sob she bent to wipe her hands on the grass—and caught a glimpse of a lone ant near the edge of the sidewalk, separated from the rest and staggering under the burden of the crumb it was carrying. The ant stopped and turned in a circle on the pavement as if unsure of its direction.

The woman sighed and stood up. She took a deep breath, feeling the air moving in and out of her body. She looked down again at the struggling ant, and then picked up a small twig from the grass. Carefully, she bent down and nudged the ant toward its fellows.

The other ants moved apart to let the wanderer into the line. Together they moved toward the crack in the sidewalk and disappeared from sight.

*

M MacKinnon writes emotions. Love, hate, fear, redemption, second chances. Her writing is primarily paranormal romance with modern mystery thrown in, and a little horror to stir the senses.

And humor. Always humor.

Monica MacKinnon's first novel in the Highland Spirits series, The Comyn's Curse, was published at the beginning of May 2019 by DarFrogPlus, and can be found in select book stores and major online sites. Please check out MacKinnon's website, https://mmackinnonwriter.com, or her Facebook author page, https://www.facebook.com/M-MacKinnon-539689769771150/?modal=admin_todo_tour.

10 MICROFICTIONS
David Ratledge

In the first minutes of battle she lost a limb. Then she lost another, and then another. The shame far outweighed the physical pain.

With only five limbs she would never be allowed to return home, but she fought on for the sake of those that still had all eight.

***

Somewhere he waits where I can't go. Not yet. But one day I will. One day it will be my time to join him, just like that horrible day when he had to leave.

He was such a good boy. Somewhere he waits patiently, a tennis ball in his mouth, knowing we will play again.

***

She carried her scars in plain sight but no one else could see them. The surface wounds had healed long ago, and had been nothing, really. The ones that mattered were deep inside, always eating at her, restraining her, changing her.

Still, she was not defeated.

***

Smoke still covered the planet. The orbital bombardment had been extreme. Clearly genocide had been the intent.

She was ready to declare it a dead world and move on, but then she heard it. Among the rubble of the largest city, faintly, she heard a baby begin to cry.

***

For a century he wandered. First one country and then another. He never stayed in one place long. Dogs immediately noticed he wasn't fully human. With people, it took longer.

She was different. She noticed right away and didn't care. For a little while he was happy.

***

The willow by the pond is where they first met. He was married. She was single, but pregnant by another. They agreed there was only one way they could spend eternity together.

They bleached their hair, moved to New Zealand, and lived happily ever after.

***

The virus was released into the world. Instead of bringing misery however, it brought empathy to all the citizens of the world. For far too many, it was a first for them.

Everything changed. Finally, world peace. Everyone now understood.

GLIMMER

***

He is the last. As he walks a decaying road through an empty place going nowhere, the ever-present dust swirls around him. It is all that remains of the billions of his people that had lived, loved, and laughed, as he once did. Still, he trudged on.

***

The acceleration was extreme, but it soon began to ease. Her dream of going to space was becoming a reality. Nobody believed she could do it. At times she had doubted it herself.

Ahead, the darkening sky filled with stars while her eyes filled with tears of joy.

***

The inferno had ravaged Earth for days, but now, only scattered small fires and dissipating smoke remained.

The survivors slowly emerged from their hidden places. Knowing the world belonged to them now, they raised their tails and began to purr.

*

David Ratledge writes micro fiction in Tennessee where he lives with his wife and cat and works full-time as an academic librarian and information technologist. He is primarily interested in science fiction but also enjoys horror and fantasy. David is part of the #vss365 writing community on Twitter.

INFINITE BLUE
Ken Carriere

Braving the heat of the scorching sun, I venture a few steps out into the ocean. The water gently laps at my knees, with a cooling effect that tries to seduce me into venturing further and deeper. This is how it tricks you. It's a seduction which leads to murder, and one I must resist. The island behind me may be my prison, but the ocean in front of me is certainly my death.

Today, like every day, the sun is merciless. It beats down relentlessly, sizzling my skin every moment I stand here. It feels like at any second I might burst into flames. I must be quick.

Squinting, and shielding my eyes with one hand, I strain my eyesight to its limit, scanning the ocean's surface for any sign of potential rescue between me and the faraway horizon.

I see something. I squint more tightly. It's the tiniest of tiny dots, possibly, just possibly, the silhouette of an unknown ship. My heart leaps. It's the first sign of human life since the shipwreck.

Has Jack's trillion-to-one shot paid off? Am I looking at the very ship that will within minutes rescue me?

Suddenly, the heat has become momentarily bearable. My toes dig into the soft ocean floor, and I stand a-tiptoe.

Then, just as suddenly as it had appeared, the distant dot disappears. Vanishes, poof, like a cruel magic trick. For several minutes, I remain in place, motionless, heartbroken and almost despairing, scanning the now empty ocean for a return of the mysterious vessel. Thoughts of doom intrude upon my mind. I have to consider the possibility that I'm doomed. Maybe this is my life now. Maybe my rescue will never come. Maybe I will die here.

The sun returns with a vengeance. Burning me, torturing me, as if angry at my ability to ignore it for a moment.

Sweating and in agony, I race back to my small shelter, and take refuge from the sun's rays. I wait, and think, and try to convince myself not to surrender to thoughts of death and doom.

This is the game I play every day of my life.

*

Roughly three weeks have passed since the shipwreck of which Jack and I had been the only survivors. Clinging to a piece of wreckage, we had floated in frigid water throughout the night, often unable to see each other despite being only a few feet apart. With no moonlight, we floated in utter darkness, until at last, just as the day broke, the current washed us ashore here — wherever "here" may be. It's a tiny island, small enough for a human to walk right around in an hour — trust me on that one. It's mostly white sand with a handful of small bushes and trees in the center. This patch of vegetation provides my shelter and also my food. Tart red berries dot the bushes, which I must be careful not to eat into extinction. The trees, meanwhile, grow small coconut, only with softer shells. Once every few days I'll crack one open. I drink the liquid inside, and consume the fleshy white lining, giving me a precious source of protein and water. Should these run out, I'd be dead within days.

No animals live on this island, thank goodness. The last thing I need is to run into a tiger. Yet I've never even seen an ant or a fly or a spider, or any type of insect for that matter. For all I know I might be the only living thing for 500 miles in every direction. Lying on my back, I stare up, through the swaying leaves, at the utterly blue sky above. You know, if the space station happens to be in orbit above me, then the astronauts on board might literally be my closest neighbors.

My thoughts drift. Hunger, heat and lack of energy put me to sleep.

*

Several hours pass and I awake, just as the sun starts to set. Its retreat gives me the chance to venture back on to the beach, and to walk without the sand scorching the bottom of my feet. It's my regular route. So many times have I taken this journey that I've subconsciously memorized every rock, every bend and twist in the land, every advance and retreat in the shoreline. Soon I'll start naming the big things. Then, the medium. If I stay here long enough, I'm sure I'll eventually name every grain of sand.

Make no mistake, this is no pleasure stroll. I have a mission. Every action must have a potentially life-saving purpose. I'm not going to let myself die here. With every step my eyes search the beach in front of me, the bushes to my right, and the ocean to my left. You might think I'm crazy. What am I going to find that I wouldn't have already found, during my previous 100 walks along this path? You might think I'm wasting my time, but I can't let myself start to think like that. I have to cling to the belief of eventual rescue as urgently as I did that shard of lifeboat. I have to believe that maybe I'll notice something new this time. Maybe today's wind has blown away enough sand to uncover something useful. Maybe today the waves will retreat just enough to expose a life-saving object sticking up from the water.

I refuse to admit I will die on this island. I reassure myself, every step brings me closer to the discovery of an escape.

GLIMMER

*

I stop for a second, and crane my neck backwards. The burnt skin makes it painful, but I do it anyway. There is not a single cloud in the sky. There almost never is. Other than the sun, the sky is nothing but blue, just infinite blue, stretching forever above me. I look at the ocean around me. It too is blue, just infinite blue, stretching forever away from me. I am the tiniest, most insignificant non-blue dot you can imagine.

I resume my walk. Halfway round the island, I stop at a bush, and eat a half-dozen of tiny, red berries which decorate its surface. Fortunately, these berries are not poisonous, at least not in the small amounts I intentionally stick to. They're not very tasty either, but they are a welcome change from leaves.

Unfortunately, my tour of the island ends without any new discovery, but I won't let a momentary disappointment collapse into an inescapable despair. I will never do that. So, I return to my shelter to think of what I can try next. There must be something I haven't thought of yet. I lie on my back, absentmindedly picking at the leaves hanging a few inches above my head, and let my drifting thoughts seek inspiration.

This is a small shelter, but of course Jack and I had no tools or supplies. Our efforts amounted to nothing more than the arrangement of a few sticks against a tree, covered it with leaves, all the while praying that a strong wind won't blow it into the water. Yes, it barely qualifies as a shelter, but it keeps the sun off my skin, and that, believe me, is all the shelter I need. Of course it's small, but it was even smaller when I had to share it with Jack.

*

Poor Jack. My thoughts turn to the day Jack lost his mind. Unlike me, utter despondency had overtaken him as it became clear no rescue would be forthcoming. His attempt to build a fire and send up a giant plume of smoke ended in utter failure, like all his other ideas had, and led to tears and screams. That afternoon, lying in the shelter, his spirit finally broke.

"I can't take it anymore!" he suddenly screamed, scaring me awake. Before I could react, he had run down to the beach, grabbed our shard of lifeboat, and, partially lying on it, started swimming out into the ocean, paddling with his hands and feet.

"Jack! Jack!" I screamed, over and over. "Come back! Jack!"

He heard me, of that there is no doubt, but chose to ignore me. There was nothing I could do but watch. Chasing after him would have meant certain death. So instead I feebly stood there, and watched as he grew smaller and smaller, until at last he vanished over the horizon.

Five or six days ago have passed since that day. I've lost count. Did he actually reach someone? I have to at least consider that possibility. It's improbable, sure, but not impossible that some passing ship picked him up. If so, then any day — any minute in fact — a rescue boat will appear. All I have to do is stay alive until it does.

I look out at the ocean. I hate it. Its power terrifies me. Death and destruction hiding beneath every wave. It can kill you so easily. Somewhere down there is my death, my destruction, just waiting, hungry, ravenous, everlastingly patient, waiting for me to make a mistake. So I won't.

*

It's morning now, barely past dawn. The sun is just starting to rise. I must have fallen asleep. My breakfast is a few leaves from a nearby bush — the word "hunger" now has a completely new meaning for me, by the way. It's just my state of existence now. Chewing on some bitter leaves which are nevertheless quite filling, I spot something

GLIMMER

floating in the ocean.

Instinctively I leap to my feet and run down to the shore. I splash out, as deep as my knees again, but dare go no further. Who knows what creatures lurk under the surface, waiting to tear me apart. Who knows how strong the current is, and how swiftly it would drag me out to my doom.

I don't need to go any further anyway. From this point, my eyes bring into focus the mystery object floating about 100 feet out. It is not, sadly, anything indicating a forthcoming rescue. Indeed, it is something which proves my rescue is further away than ever. It is Jack, floating face down, arms outstretched. His corpse bobs on the waves as if it were a log or some other piece of worthless garbage. It's an obscene and sickening sight. He never stood a chance.

For a moment I consider swimming out and retrieving him, but — I hate to say it — he's still too far out and it's not worth the risk.

I'm sorry, Jack. I'm so, so sorry.

*

Trying not to surrender to my darkest thoughts, I steel myself in the face of death. I will NOT give up. I don't care if there is one leaf left and I don't care if 20 years pass. I don't care if all my attempts fail and I don't care how much pain I'm in. I will not give up. I will NEVER give up. I will find a way off. I will find a way to rescue myself.

I just have to think of how.

*

Suddenly, I see something. In the sky, far away, no more than a speck but definitely an airplane.

Instinctively I start jumping and screaming, waving both arms so furiously I might take flight myself.

"Hey!" I shout. "Heyyyyyy!"

There's no way they can hear me, of course. I'm wasting

GLIMMER

time. But I have a better chance!

I race back to the shelter. Wrapped in a few leaves is my cellphone, which had been in my pocket when we came ashore. Of course, the water destroyed it, and even if it had by some miracle retained some power, there'd be no signal. Should I die here, and my body rot into nothing, then this phone will be the sole testament of my existence here. You want a signal? It will send a signal throughout eternity that I was here.

Morbid philosophies can wait. For now, I have an idea which might just work. In eagerness I seize the phone and race back to the shore, at the point of island closest to the airplane.

Maybe, just maybe, I can reflect the sunlight off the screen — it's the only shiny object in my possession — and catch the pilot's attention. I wade out into the water, waist deep, deeper than I've ever dared before. Bravery mixed with recklessness control my actions. The plane must be several miles off, but my heart urges me to get as close as possible. Every extra inch will help bridge the gap between rescue and continued exile, between the pilot seeing nothing and the pilot spotting just the tiniest, curious glimmer at the furthest reaches of his vision. Every inch — every partial inch — counts. I stretch my arm up high, reaching my phone's screen as far as my arm will go, but it's no good. The plane continues on its uninterrupted path. Worse still, I realize, as it disappears and I turn back to the island, the sun had been behind me all this time. No light could have ever reflected off the screen.

I force myself to stay positive. This was a worthwhile attempt. It taught me something for my next attempt, and maybe my next attempt will bring me more luck. The plane will be a little closer. The sun will be in a better position. And I'll get that extra half-inch closer.

*

GLIMMER

After tucking the cellphone away, rewrapped in leaves, I decide to walk around the beach, before the sun gets too high in the sky and the heat becomes unbearable again. This time, I do find something useful. On the other side of the island, there's a half-buried rock, which of course I've passed many times before. I've never paid it much attention. It is flat and seems to be useless, when it occurs to me to give it closer attention. On my hands and knees, I dig the sand away from its buried side edge, and discover that here it is thin and tapers to a point. It's not super-sharp, like a knife or an ax-head would be, but perhaps it will prove sharp enough. Maybe I can use it to chop up a few bushes, or dig up some other stones and spell out the word "HELP" on the beach.

In fact, I don't need to spell out the whole word, do I? Surely just a single letter on a supposedly uninhabited island would grab a pilot's attention?

*

I've thought of two good ideas and it isn't even noon. How's that for not giving up? I tell you, I will get rescued. I will. There must be a way to escape my horrible situation. I only need to figure it out.

Carrying my new stone, I head back to my shelter, before the heat gets unbearable.

I lie down, smiling and with a happy heart, and through the leaves stare up at the clear sky. I turn my head and stare out at the empty water. Yesterday, I was here. Today, I'm still here. Tomorrow, well tomorrow, I may still be here, but one day, and one day soon, I will escape the infinite blue.

*

GLIMMER

Ken Carriere works in IT in Toronto, Canada. His primary source of education has been accidentally breaking things and then needing to learn how to fix them before anyone finds out, which is exactly what's going on at his website, www.kencar.com

A WOODSTOCK WISH
Des Dixon

In the summer of 1969, young Randy Rockwood was a stockbroker, a very lucrative job. It was quite an accomplishment but he hated it and told friends, "I wish I could chuck this job and live the simple life of an honest farmer."

On a slack Monday morning, he left his office for a coffee and bought a copy of Rolling Stone magazine. Randy flipped through until he saw the following ad,

WOODSTOCK ROCK CONCERT! Rock Music Festival August 23-26, 1969 in upstate NY featuring Joan Baez, Santana, the Grateful Dead, Creedence Clearwater Revival, Janis Joplin, Sly, and the Family Stone, The Who, Jefferson Airplane, The Band, Crosby, Stills, Nash & Young, and Jimi Hendrix. Tickets, details at your music store.

For the next few months, he planned his three-day escape, bought a ticket, and then purchased a new Volkswagen Van. He didn't realize there would be over half a million fans including hippies making that historical trek to Woodstock.

It was time to go and he packed a cooler of sandwiches and soft-drinks then set his sights north. When he reached Albany he swung West to complete the final leg to the Rome, NY area where the concert was being held. He noticed many hitch-hikers on the road but was reluctant to pick them up as many were stoned on drugs or LSD.

Then he saw a beautiful girl hitch-hiking and smiling at him. She had class, style, and beauty all in one package and

GLIMMER

Randy jammed on his brakes.

"Do you want a lift?"

"Sure do, providing you're not high on drugs or alcohol or not a pervert!"

"You're pretty and not too humble for a hitchhiker, but no, on both counts."

She got in and scrutinized Randy and held the door open ready for a quick exit.

"I'm not fussy but I don't want my life to end for making the wrong choice."

"Pretty girl, you made the wrong choice when you decided to hitchhike."

"Well, everybody hitchhikes these days so I wanted to see what it was like."

"I get it, an adventure for a princess so she can rub elbows with commoners."

"Something like that, a little rich girl with a sheltered life until she broke out."

"Hey, you're saying you got money and you shouldn't tell anyone that stuff!"

"Thanks, I'm Fiona Feeney from Boston, and I'm beginning to like you."

"Randy Rockwood, NYC, and a stockbroker but looking at other options."

"I know what you mean Randy, I'm looking for a way out myself."

"Hey, Fiona this is gonna be a blast but it's too bad Lead Zeppelin has opted out because of other commitments."

"Ya, but I'm looking forward to Joni Mitchell as her lyrics carry a message and make you think of where society is going. Isn't that right Randy?"

"Ya, I guess, but I just like to get lost in the music and not think about stuff."

"Come on Randy, don't say you're a mindless airhead cause you're not."

"Not fair, Fiona, as you got me pegged as a tight-assed, buttoned-up city-slicker but I'm gonna prove to you that

GLIMMER

you're wrong."

"How are you gonna do that Randy?"

"I'm gonna steal you from your Daddy's mansion and carry you away to my hovel. There I will transform you from riches to rags. We would have lived happily but Daddy found us and paid the Sherriff to put me in jail for life."

"Wow! That sounds like you have designs on me and it was almost a proposal."

"Ya, I guess it nearly was but your Daddy's probably got half the Boston Police Department after that bounder who lured his princess away. "

"You're talkin' big Mr. City Slicker but you're movin' too fast for this here smalltown gal."

"No, I'm not, I'm just kiddin' and beneath this fast-talker is a very shy guy."

"I like shy guys as long as they stay that way."

Randy and Fiona bantered back and forth sparring with each other on all subjects from their likes or dislikes of music, sports, food, and people.

The long trip went by quickly and they were suddenly there at Woodstock!

They mingled with the crowd until they found a good place to enjoy the venues.

Randy stared at Fiona's tall, slender figure, and her long black hair with a blunt cut at her forehead.

They were among the hundreds of thousands who were mesmerized by the lineup of talent and as the night wore on Fiona couldn't keep her eyes open.

"Joni Mitchell's a no-show so I'm gonna pitch a tent'n crash."

"Hey, I wouldn't do that as people are drinkin' and smokin' pot. Why don't you sleep in my van and I'll sleep in the front cab."

"Sounds good Randy 'cause I'm really beat."

They were together for three days and nights and then Woodstock was over. Jimi Hendrix was the last one on stage and completed his performance by pouring lighter fluid on the guitar and setting it on fire.

The musicians went on to fame and the crowds drifted into obscurity. Randy and Fiona stayed an extra night. They huddled together in the dark and the only the sounds were the chirp of the crickets and the hoot of an owl.

They gazed at the stars and couldn't face tomorrow when they would say their goodbyes and perhaps never meet again.

Fiona couldn't hold back her tears and said, "I'm going to wish on a star Randy so hold my hand, look at the brightest star, so here goes... Starlight star bright the first star I see tonight. I wish I may, I wish I might have the wish I wish tonight." They both wished never to part.

When they were at their lowest ebb Randy said to Fiona, "I want to spend the rest of my life with you Fiona, so let's chuck it all and do our own thing. We'll go up to the Vermont woods, build a log cabin and have a garden, chickens, a goat for milk. and we'll go back to the land." "Do you mean it, Randy, you're willing to give up your promising career'"

They built their log cabin deep in the Vermont forest and lived the life of pioneers. Randy dug a garden plot and Fiona planted cabbage, onions, carrots, and potatoes. In early Spring they started some of the vegetables in boxes within their cabin as it was a short growing season.

"Fiona there are holes in the leaves of plants in our garden!" Randy yelled.

"Yes, Randy, I noticed it too and read up on it in that gardening book we got at Hank's General Store in that little village of Cobblers Corners. If you look at the back of those leaves you will see little green aphids eating away. The book says to cover the back of the leaves with soapy water as it is a harmless substitute for poisonous chemicals."

Their love for each other endured and withstood the test of time. Woodstock faded into a distant memory and their love affair grew even stronger when Fiona had a stroke just after her seventy-third birthday celebration.

Randy moved Fiona's bed near his easy chair and the pot-belly stove. He got up every night, lifted the stove lid, poked

GLIMMER

the embers into a flame, then added some wood. He washed her bedclothes in rainwater and used the lye soap he and Fiona made from hardwood ashes, meat fat, and rainwater.

Fiona grew restless then settled down and Andy fell asleep in his chair. He woke up during the night and it was strangely quiet and peaceful. He bent over Fiona and listened but she wasn't breathing and her forehead was cold. He couldn't conceive that she had left him all alone. She took part of him with her.

As he gazed in disbelief at her still and beautiful face he heard Fiona say, "Isn't that right Randy?" It was a phrase she often used. He realized he would never hear her voice again. It was more than he could bear and like a stab in the heart.

Randy broke down sobbing like a little boy until all his emotions were spent. He looked back to the day they first met and the time when their love was new. He snapped back to the present and his thoughts returned to Fiona and how much he loved her and missed her.

He wrapped Fiona in a blanket and carried her out to the grave he dug but loved her too much to put her under the ground. He carried her body back in the cabin then held her in his arms as he sat in his chair

Later that February two Game Wardens found Randy still sitting there in his chair holding Fiona and both bodies were frozen.

He left his hand-written will, donating their log cabin the County. He also left instructions for them to sprinkle their ashes beside the garden where he and Fiona watched the sunset in the evening.

The log cabin that Randy and Fiona built is now a way station and refuge for Game Wardens or those who travel the woodlands.

*

FAMILY
Des Dixon

I led a lonely life and would have wed a homely wife.
But I found my honey and she didn't care about money.
She was to be the life of my love and the love of my life.
Our lives we would share and we made a peach of a pair.

We lived, we laughed, we loved, just like two turtledoves.
Not like Jack and Jill as we didn't have a house on the hill.
What we were after was a house of kids, fun, and laughter.
A house with both joy and laughter is all we were ever after.

I had a good home with a wife who would never, ever, roam.
She stayed the course through both our good times or worse.
Four children, we had through both good times and the bad.
But love conquered all as our brood grew up healthy and tall.

Her pies became a fable, the boys invited all kids to our table.
"Son, this ain't Meals-On-Wheels, it's all hard work by Mom."
Sunday fare when we all sat to eat and it was always a treat.
Never thanks were given but she smiled and all was forgiven.

That's it, that was our day, and I'm not out-to-lunch when I say,
"You did it, honey, you kept us afloat and the Captain of our
boat."
Remember the walks in the park, sleigh rides, dances in the dark?
We had fun when the kids were young, we had a ball, you did it all.

*

Des Dixon was the oldest member of this writing group and a veteran of the Royal Canadian Air Force. The second picture shows his brother Jim on the far right, in 1943. Des had many adventures in his life including working as a Miner, a Forest Ranger, and a Fishing Guide.

He also worked as an Air Surveyor, and a Commercial Real Estate Agent, in addition to his twenty-two years in the RCAF. Des was a member of The Write Practice writers club 2017-2020.

THE DINOSAURS
E. C. Haskell

"Hey, cuz! Does this mean I'm off your shit list?"

With a foolish grin, I collapsed onto my leather sofa, sending dust motes dancing through the late afternoon light. I hadn't heard from my favorite cousin, Clara, in nearly seven months and that wasn't like her. Still, after that scene at our family cemetery, I probably should have expected it. But I had apologized. Even sent her a funny birthday card.

Nothing worked. Which pissed me off because it really wasn't all my fault. It had been late October and I'd flown to New York for the internment of Clara's mother, my Aunt Jo. I got to Sag Harbor a little late and was hurrying along the path to the Irving graveyard, thinking about my Aunt. She'd been a reserved woman, shy really, and a bit embarrassed by Clara's endless fascination with the Irving blue-blooded lineage.

So I was wondering why Aunt Jo would choose to be buried in the family plot. It just wasn't her style. Of course, it could have been more Clara's decision and anyway, when you get put down for eternal rest, you might as well be nestled among tupelo trees with the graves of relatives going back to the late sixteen-hundreds all around you.

But I was late. I hurried through the ancient cast-iron gate, made a dash toward the sound of voices and walked smack dab into a hallucination. At least that's what I hoped it was. Before me was a mahogany casket, an open grave and beyond that a marble headstone approximately the size and

GLIMMER

shape of an eighteen wheeler's front end. Josephine Cordelia Irving was engraved in the center of the marble expanse. And all around were the names of famous Irving ancestors, lifespans and honorifics included.

If she wasn't already dead, Aunt Jo would have passed from sheer embarrassment. I guess I must have muttered something about that because, before I could take another step, Clara walloped me in the solar plexus with her Dagne Dover tote. I choked and yelled a few words I shouldn't have. The other people at the gravesite – all seven of them – averted their eyes. They spent most of the service pretending we were invisible.

Clara hadn't spoken to me since. Now, however, she seemed to have called. Or at least her breathing had.

"So ... did you call just to let me know that we're still not speaking?"

More silence. And then a gulp of air followed by the snort of a sob.

Now that made me sit right up. "Clara?"

"S-sorry." Her voice dragged, ending with a hiccup.

"What's wrong?" I asked.

"Everything."

"Wow." Getting up from the couch, I wandered over to my floor-to-ceiling window with its view of Coors field, the haze of west Denver and, in the far distance, the purple peaks of the Rocky Mountains. Solace in scenery is among my many mantras. It wasn't helping. "Want to start with the state of the world and winnow it down from there?"

The hiss of indrawn breath told me that my foot had once again found my mouth. I gave myself a mental slap and tried to soften my voice. "Talk to me Clara."

She took a deep breath. "It's Courtney!"

Oh shit. There wasn't enough scenery in the world to deal with this one. "What's she done now?"

"She ... she's d-dying."

At first I thought she was joking but the sound of sobbing put a damper on that. Still, Courtney Irving dying?

Clara's sister had been in college when Clara and I were still in middle school and, to me, she'd always seemed invincible. A statuesque blonde who drew men like ants to a picnic, she possessed the elegance of a ballerina, a famously dry wit and the instincts of a velociraptor. In short, she scared the shit out of me. But dying? No.

"She has stomach cancer," Clara said. "Stage four. She tried all kinds of treatment but ... well, now she's back home. J-Joel's staying with her."

Courtney's ex-husband, a talented musician, was one of the few things I really liked about her.

"That's good. Right?"

"I guess. But ...."

I divined a favor in the offing. "What do you need?" I spoke tentatively, as if I were wading into a minefield. Which I pretty much was.

She answered with a gulp. "Can you send her something? Please?"

"Like what?"

"Doesn't matter. She's scared, Nan! And even with Joel there she feels so alone. I think she needs family. It would mean so much if she could get a package from you."

"Sure," I said, although the thought of shopping for a dying velociraptor made my lips pucker.

"Oh god, thank you." Clara sounded genuinely relieved. "Oh and Nan?"

"Yes?"

"Do it quickly."

So there it was. An urgent need to find a present for a woman whose last words to me had been something along the lines of 'I'd say you're a bitch but I don't want to be complimentary".

Insane, but Clara and I had virtually grown up together. And Courtney .... Well, she was family too. Besides, I'd always kind of admired her.

I started with the idea of flowers. But that's what you send to funerals and I knew that Clara wanted Courtney to get a gift while still alive. Or how about a nice bed jacket? Mmm ... tacky. Emphasizes that she'll never be getting out of bed. Personally I thought I'd want about a pound of fudge. Tastes great and dieting wouldn't be an issue. But Courtney might take that the wrong way.

Then it hit me. Something silly. The sillier the better.

That's what I'd done years earlier when my father was very ill. Hoping to cheer him up, I started sending silly things. A stuffed zebra that I dubbed High Hopes. A book of the world's worst jokes. A red-nosed reindeer that sang a drinking song. (He played it for all his nurses.)

He told me that those silly things made him laugh so that's what I'd try to do for Courtney. Of course, finding a truly silly thing is not easy. Kind of like hunting for a unicorn in the London Zoo: you're not sure it exists but you still hope it's there. It took me several days but finally, one smog-choked evening, I spotted it in the window of a Dollar store: a stuffed Triceratops with fluffy fur the color of Cheetos, big brown eyes and a black nose that squeaked.

Perfect.

I took it home, wrapped it in gaily colored tissue and found a box.

Two days later I still hadn't mailed it. Call it the gloom of an unusually rainy May or the buried remains of my conscience but I knew that dinosaur wasn't quite enough.

So I sat down. Stared at my computer for the better part of an hour. And began to write a letter.

I wrote about how our once large and distinguished clan had been whittled down by the centuries and how deeply I treasured her presence in it. I wrote about memories from family vacations when Clara, Courtney and I skinny-dipped in beaver ponds and short-sheeted each other's beds. I wrote about her father who passed years earlier and how I noticed her holding Clara's hand throughout his service. But most of all I wrote about love and how it can endure through stupid fights, silly slights and missed chances. Somehow, in that writing, a caring that I didn't know I had

GLIMMER

leaked out, and so, to my embarrassment, did tears.

Sappy? You bet. And I had a fine old argument with myself about sending it. But Courtney didn't have long so I packed that letter up, along with the orange dinosaur and all that happy colored paper.

I didn't hear anything back. Well, what did I expect? My distant family, with its distinguished lineage and the ice of ancient aristocracy in its veins, was hardly the communicating type. I tried not to let that bother me.

But then I got another call from Clara. Courtney was gone. We spoke for over an hour but it wasn't until we were ready to sign off that I asked the question that had been haunting me. Did Courtney get the dinosaur and my letter?

"Oh lord," Clara laughed, "that dinosaur."

"It didn't piss her off?"

"No! On my last visit to her, I asked if she'd heard from you. She nodded. She couldn't speak by then so Joel jumped in and said you wrote a really nice letter. I asked if you'd sent anything with the letter. Courtney smiled. Her hands began to move under the covers. She pushed them aside and there was that dinosaur, cuddled in her arm."

It was then that I understood what I'd been missing so long. The warmth that can underlie even the most fractured family relationship. And the real value of those relationships when the world seems torn asunder. Which is why the very next day I went to that Dollar Store and bought another orange dinosaur. A stegosaurus this time. I wrapped it in that bright tissue paper, made a copy of the letter I'd written to Courtney and sent it all to Clara with a short note.

"This one's for you."

*

GLIMMER

Evie Haskell is a writer/editor who has produced everything from advertisements to magazine articles, in-depth technology reports, adventure articles and, of course, enews letters and blogs. Most recently she has turned her attention to fiction where she is exploring the worlds of media, advanced technologies and the implications of quantum physics. She is currently working on a novel, Harbinger. Flickerings is among her first short stories.

Evie lives in Breckenridge, Colorado with her family, two dogs and an assorted cast of coyotes, foxes, moose and bears.

A WAKE NO LONGER
J.H. O'Rourke

Heart racing, she closed her eyes against the frigid wind, the pounding waves.

Was it mere hours since she sat on the deck chair, the sunshine warming her nape? Mere hours since she wrapped the tiny replica in delicate tissue paper and carefully scrawled 'To Mother, With Love'?

"Hello?" a man's voice echoed.

Her eyes snapped open. "Over here!"

Cold, dead flesh grazed her arm and she screamed.

A bright light momentarily blinded her.

"I'll be right there," assured the voice.

As the lifeboat drifted closer, she gaped in horror as the Titanic disappeared into the depths of the ocean.

*

UNCONDITIONAL
J.H. O'Rourke

Jason's bed is so comfortable. It's the first I've ever shared with a man. My heart swells with love as I recall resting my head on his chest last night, his fingers caressing my neck, my back.

Stretching and yawning, I open my eyes. I can't read the time on the alarm clock but can tell by the direction of the sun shining in through the lace curtains that it's late morning. I just couldn't resist going back to bed after seeing Jason off to work this morning.

After bathing as well as I'm able to in my restricted state, I limp to the kitchen for a bite to eat.

My leg feels much better, but the cast itches like crazy. Whenever Jason catches me trying to dig my nails underneath to scratch, he places his warm hand on my leg and gently urges me to stop.

I hope the doctor removes the damn thing soon.

Jason prepared my breakfast before leaving, as he always does. The savory scent of bacon entices me as I sniff the air. I try not to eat too quickly; I now know there will be more food later.

After satisfying my hunger, I head for the window seat in the living room. It offers the best view of the front yard. I enjoy watching birds soaring overhead, squirrels scurrying along tree branches, and people walking down the street. Not the cats though; I've never liked them.

It seems as if there's an endless parade of them walking

down the sidewalk or across the street. How annoying! Where do they all come from? Whenever one dares to saunter across our front yard, I yell at it to get off our property. I wish I could just chase them all away!

There is beauty in the contrast between the bright-red fire hydrant and the lush green grass of early spring. Although I've always experienced difficulty distinguishing colors, I can easily spot the yellow dandelions peppering the lawn. I envision relaxing outside and napping under the rays of the sun.

I acknowledge the mailman as he makes his delivery. He never says a word to me. Instead, he just stares at my leg with an expression I can only describe as a combination of fear and relief, which doesn't make sense.

I'm not expecting any other visitors, so I shuffle back to the window seat. Of course, I'll drag myself back to the door to greet anyone who happens to knock throughout the day, or even steps onto the property for that matter. I may even shout out to strangers who walk past the house through the window.

If I end up falling asleep again, I know with certainty I'll hear Jason's car the moment it pulls into the driveway. His return is all I think about. I love him so much.

I'm happy for the first time in my life. My only wish is that I can stay.

*

By the time I met Jason, I'd hit rock bottom. I had nowhere to live, hadn't eaten more than a few scraps of food in days, and had no friends or family. I was alone and struggling every single day simply to survive.

It was so cold out it felt as if my bones had frozen and my blood had turned to ice. My sister Sandy and I had been kicked out of the warehouse we'd been squatting in nearly a month earlier.

After several nights spent sleeping behind a garbage

dumpster in an effort to hide from the wind and snow, I woke up and Sandy was just... gone.

Had someone abducted her?

Had she been searching for food and gotten lost on her way back?

Or something worse?

Could Sandy have met the same fate as our mother? I hate thinking about it. Mom had been hit by a car a year earlier. I doubt the driver even slowed down, let alone stopped. He or she most likely acted as if nothing had happened and just left Mom's twisted, bleeding body on the side of the road. By the time Sandy and I found her, she was dead. Not one person offered to help us or even seemed to care. Not one.

Then, after Sandy disappeared, I'd walk the streets at night and sneak food from garbage cans behind restaurants. Occasionally, someone took pity on me and offered me something to eat. During the coldest nights, I'd curl up beneath someone's porch or slip into a shed to shield myself from the elements, but the owners often caught me and insisted I leave. I finally gave up trying and returned to my make-shift home behind the dumpster.

And I never stopped thinking maybe, just maybe, Sandy would come back for me. But she never did.

I watched Jason walk by my hiding place every day for nearly a week before he noticed me. He always wore a hooded winter jacket that masked his features and a pair of warm-looking boots. I'd never owned boots. Or even a jacket for that matter.

The first time he approached me, my fight-or-flight instinct had kicked in. I would have made a run for it if I hadn't hurt my leg the night before. I'd been startled into tripping down a set of stairs by an upset store owner for rifling through his garbage.

Jason introduced himself and asked me questions about myself and my situation, but I didn't answer. Instead, I cowered and whimpered in fear. I expected him to pretend to act nice but then hit and kick me. Or scream at me and call me names. So when he took off his coat and wrapped it around my shoulders, I just stared at him, confused and speechless.

What would he expect in return?

The following day, I didn't recognize Jason at first and struggled to move away from him when he stopped and knelt beside me. But his soothing voice assured me he was, in fact, the same kind man who had cared enough about a homeless stranger to give me his jacket.

He reached into his pocket and pulled out two breakfast sandwiches. He handed one to me. I just stared at it at first. Was he just teasing me? Would he take it back when I reached for it? When Jason insisted I take it, I grabbed it and scarfed it down, barely tasting it. It was the first real meal I'd had for weeks. I noticed Jason taking delicate bites of his own and hung my head in shame and embarrassment. He didn't seem to notice. Instead, he reached over and pulled the jacket he had given me tight around my shoulders, warming me inside and out. Then he stood, told me he'd see me again soon, and continued on his way to work.

My leg felt worse the next morning. A lot worse. I had spent the night vomiting and, for the first time since Jason had given it to me, slipped his jacket off my shoulders. I was burning up despite the snow and cold wind.

Jason noticed immediately.

He took out his cell phone and called his workplace to let them know he'd be late, then hailed a taxi. I didn't have the energy to protest when Jason gently picked me up and placed me in the back of the car. He sat in the front seat and told the driver to take us to the hospital.

Jason stuck around while the doctor took an x-ray, then diagnosed me with a fractured bone and an infection. She placed a cast on my leg, prescribed some antibiotics, and told me I'd be fine. That's when Jason explained I had nowhere to live. The doctor told us I couldn't recover properly on the streets and picked up the phone to call a shelter. Jason stopped her and turned to me. He told me he had lots of room in his house and asked if I'd like to stay with him until my leg had healed.

I stared at him wide-eyed, so surprised by his proposition that his words didn't register at first. Was this man, this stranger, really willing to take me in and look after me? Could I have misunderstood?

But Jason meant what he said. In a matter of hours I had moved from behind a garbage bin into a real house. And it was the first time in my adult life I felt as if someone truly cared.

It didn't take long before I fell in love with him. I could tell by the look in his eyes he was falling for me too.

A month went by before I got up the courage to leave the spare bedroom late one night and enter Jason's. I just wanted to look at him.

No, I'm lying.

I wanted to lie beside him, to cuddle with him, to feel his arms around me. He looked up from the book he was reading. I felt mortified, surprised he was still awake. Instead of telling me to go away, he patted the opposite side of the bed and invited me to join him.

I've slept next to him every night since.

*

The itching underneath my cast wakes me from my nap. I glance out the window and begin to get excited. It's late afternoon; Jason will return before too long.

My hope is that, after I've fully recovered, Jason will want to continue our relationship. I can't imagine my life without him. I pray he feels the same way.

We never talk about what will happen once my leg is healed. I hope he doesn't ask me to leave as soon as I'm better. It's my greatest fear.

In the beginning, the clear plan was for me to stay temporarily until I feel well enough to take care of myself without Jason's help. But we were mere acquaintances at the time. We're so much more now.

Jason is the first person who's made me feel as if I matter. He's the first person who hasn't hurt me. He is the one person I want to spend the rest of my life with.

What's that noise? Who's shouting? I cringe at the sound. I'm used to being the one yelled at, screamed at, told that I'm 'bad'. I glare out the window at the kids walking past the house on their way home from school. I call to them, telling them to stay off the lawn. They stare back at me. A couple of them point; others greet me in kind voices. No one laughs or says anything mean. I'm still not used to this kind of treatment after all these weeks.

Eventually, the groups of children dwindle down, replaced by cars driven by those heading home from work. Jason should be here soon. I tremble with excitement and force myself to relax.

The minutes seem like hours as I wait.

Finally, I am rewarded by the distinct sound of Jason's car pulling into the driveway. I welcome him home through the window. He smiles at me and holds up a container. I recognize the logo as being from the store that sells my favorite food.

My pulse pounds with anticipation as I hobble from the window seat to the front door, eagerly listening to the jingle of Jason's keys as he unlocks, then opens the door.

"Hey, you! I hope you had a good day!" He motions to the bag in his hand. "I brought you a little treat."

He bends down to accept my kiss of appreciation and embraces me.

"I consider it a celebration," he tells me. "A housewarming gift, actually."

A housewarming gift? Could it be? My breath quickens.

Jason looks into my eyes. "I know we had planned you would live here just until you're all better, but I want you to stay. I love you and promise to protect and take care of you. I hope you want that too."

GLIMMER

I nuzzle his neck; I kiss his cheek and mouth in response. I'm shaking all over. I want this more than anything!

Jason laughs. "I'll take that as a 'yes'! Welcome to your forever home!"

Jason reaches into the closet and pulls out my leash. He attaches it to my collar.

"How about a nice, slow walk around the block before supper, Rex?"

I wag my tail in agreement.

*

J. H. O'Rourke is a published writer and editor from Nova Scotia, Canada, eh? She is the author of numerous short stories, many of which have won awards and contests. Ms. O'Rourke enjoys devising creepy plot twists that explore the darkness of the human mind and enticing her readers to sleep with the lights on. Her debut full-length psychological thriller Mind Crawlers is due for publication in 2020. Ms. O'Rourke actively participates in several writing groups and is an avid reader and critiquer.

Visit her website https://jenhorganorourke.com/, *Like her Facebook Author Page and follow her on Twitter to learn more about the author and her writing journey.*

GLIMMER

GLIMMER

ABOUT THE AUTHORS

The writers in this anthology mostly met through the online writing community, The Write Practice, run by Joe Bunting. The Write Practice encourages writers to form a solid writing habit: share a piece of work each week and provide actionable critique on others' work. This habit has led to friendships and the confidence to reach out to other writers – some contributors met in the Twitter #vss365 community, or at real-life open mic sessions.

Every writer is at a different stage in their career, but supports the rest of the group with feedback, suggestions, and encouragement.

We urge every writer to find their writing community.